Tall Tales of Tenali Ramakrishna

RED
PANDA

Tall Tales of Tenali Ramakrishna

lesser-known stories and secret adventures

Retold by PURNIMA RAMAKRISHNAN

Illustrated by ENAKSHI GOSWAMI

Published by Red Panda, an imprint of Westland Books, a division of Nasadiya Technologies Private Limited, in 2025

No. 269/2B, First Floor, 'Irai Arul', Vimalraj Street, Nethaji Nagar, Alapakkam Main Road, Maduravoyal, Chennai 600095

Westland, the Westland logo, Red Panda and the Red Panda logo are the trademarks of Nasadiya Technologies Private Limited, or its affiliates.

ISBN: 9789371972178

10 9 8 7 6 5 4 3

Book design by Mukul Chand

Printed at Thomson Press (India) Ltd

To Daaji,

who recognised the stories in my heart before
I could pen them down,
who placed storytelling in service of consciousness,
as wit, wisdom, love and laughter are tools to awaken the spirit.

This book is offered in that light, for the children of today, and
the child in every reader.

Contents

Riddle Me This, Raja!
Where questions are curiouser, and answers curiouser still.

Common Sense, Uncommon Wins!
When sharp thinking trumps shiny swords.

Author's Note

Dear Readers

This is not just another book of Tenali Raman stories. This book is special. This book is unique. Why? Because this collection of tales is meant for more than just entertainment. These stories are your guide to thinking more sharply, acting more wisely and navigating the world with confidence and humour, just like Tenali Raman did.

So, who was Tenali Raman?

Some call him the Birbal of the south, but that comparison only scratches the surface. While both Birbal and Tenali Raman were brilliant courtiers known for their quick wit and wisdom, they differed in many ways. Birbal's intelligence came wrapped in diplomacy and careful reasoning, while Tenali Raman's brilliance was sharper, playful and sometimes mischievous. He used humour and unconventional thinking to outsmart his opponents.

Born as Ramakrishna in a small village, Tenali's journey was not easy. He had no formal education, no noble birthright, no wealth. And yet, he rose to become the trusted adviser of one of the greatest kings in Indian history, Krishnadevaraya of Vijayanagara, and the most fascinating figure in Indian folklore. A wise and visionary ruler, Krishnadevaraya led the Vijayanagara empire to its golden age, encouraging art, literature and intellect in his court. It was in this vibrant atmosphere that Tenali's brilliance truly shone.

What makes these stories so important?

Many stories like *Aesop's Fables* or the *Panchatantra* were written to teach lessons about life. But Tenali Raman's stories? They are not fables. They are history. These incidents truly took place. And through them, we learn something truly valuable.

- How to outsmart a liar.
- How to turn the tables on greed and corruption.
- How to survive even the trickiest of situations using nothing but intelligence and humour.

Tenali Raman's sharp mind was his greatest weapon, and his heart his greatest guide. He proved that wisdom is about knowing what to do at the right moment.

Why is this book called Tenali 'Ramakrishna'?

You might have seen other books simply call him Tenali Raman, but this one uses his true name in the title—Ramakrishna.

Since ancient times in India, Krishna has been a name that represents wisdom, strategy, playfulness and balance. Tenali Raman carried forward this legacy, blending laughter with insight and humour with devotion. He never forgot his roots. He remained humble, alert and always one step ahead of those who tried to deceive him.

Though this book is titled using his real name 'Tenali Ramakrishna', you'll notice we affectionately call him Tenali or Tenali Raman throughout. Why is that?

Because that's how he is best remembered. Over the centuries, his stories have travelled far and wide, across generations and geographies, and the name 'Tenali Raman' has become part of everyday storytelling, from classrooms to family gatherings. So while we honour Ramakrishna in the title, within these tales, we'll call him the way the world fondly remembers him.

So, as you turn the pages, remember this:

Tenali Raman was not born powerful. He became powerful by using his mind. He never needed swords. His words were sharper than any blade. And he never forgot to laugh, even when life tested him.

Are you ready to outthink the powerful, outsmart the cunning and see the world with the wit and wisdom of Tenali Raman?

Then, let's begin.

Purnima Ramakrishnan
June 2025

Courtroom Coconuts!

Where royal justice gets
a hilarious knock
on the head.

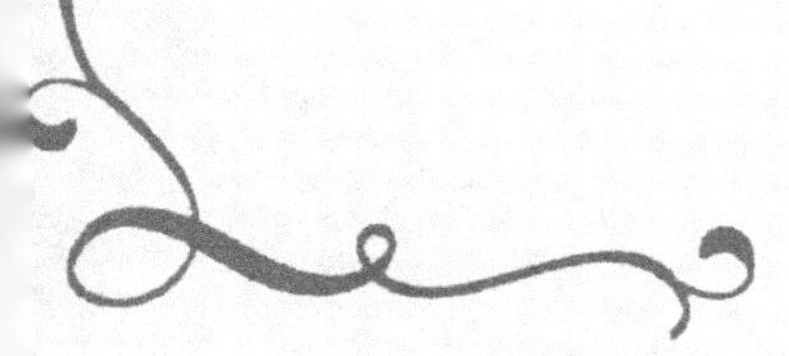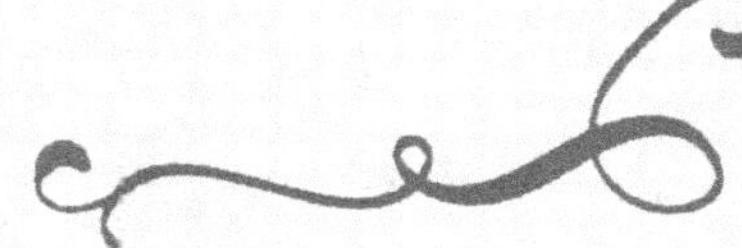

1

Bitten by the Apple, Saved by Wit

The royal garden was like a hidden treasure trove.

It was lush green, glowing under the moonlight and filled with trees bearing shimmering golden apples. These apples were so rare that merchants from Persia paid a fortune for just one bite.

And, of course, where there's treasure, there are guards. The king had his best men patrolling the orchard, their torches flickering like watchful eyes, ensuring that not a single apple was stolen.

But the sweetest fruits are often the most tempting.

One evening, after a lavish royal feast, King Krishnadevaraya was unusually generous. He leaned

forward and handed four golden apples to his most trusted courtier, Tenali Raman.

'A little gift for you,' the king said.

Tenali took them home and placed them on the table. But his young nephew, a curious village boy with a never-ending appetite, stared at them like a cat eyeing a bowl of fish.

Just one bite, he told himself. But the moment he sank his teeth into the juicy fruit, his eyes widened. Its taste was like golden sunshine melting on his tongue. And just like that one apple wasn't enough. He finished all four!

Temptation gnawed at him. If he could have one, why not more? *Why stop at four?*

That night, when the moon hid behind the clouds, he tiptoed past the towering palace gates, his heart pounding like a drum. The orchard was eerily silent except for the rustling of leaves and his own racing heartbeat.

One apple, two, three—soon, his bag was stuffed with stolen treasure.

Then, CRACK!

A dry branch snapped beneath his foot.

'Who's there?' a guard's voice sliced through the silence.

Before the boy could react, the glow of flaming torches flared, shadows flickered and footsteps thundered towards him. In the blink of an eye, he was caught.

The next morning, he stood before King Krishnadevaraya.

'Stealing from the king himself?' The king's booming voice shook the courtroom. 'The law is equal for all! Throw him in jail!'

The boy's face drained of colour. Just yesterday he was biting into a golden apple, and now, he was staring at a lifetime behind iron bars.

WHAT WOULD YOU DO IF YOU WERE THE BOY?
* Would you try to escape?
* Would you come up with a clever trick like Tenali Raman?

Soon, word reached Tenali Raman. He sprinted to the palace, his turban nearly flying off.

'Tenali,' the king warned, crossing his arms, 'don't even try your usual tricks. This time, I've already made my decision. I'll make it simple. Whatever you ask for, I will do the opposite!'

Not a sound stirred in the vast hall. Even the ministers stopped fanning themselves. Tenali bowed gracefully, then smiled ever so slightly.

'In that case, Your Majesty,' he said calmly, 'I ask you to give my nephew the harshest punishment possible—life imprisonment. Do not show him even a shred of mercy!'

The king's hand froze mid-air. The courtiers whispered in confusion. The minister gasped.

'Your Majesty! Tenali has outwitted you again! If you must do the opposite of what he says, you have to set the boy free!'

The king's brows furrowed. He looked at Tenali. He looked at the minister. He looked at the boy. Then, he threw his head back and roared with laughter.

'Very well! You win, Tenali!' he declared. He turned to the boy, shaking his head. 'Your uncle saved you today, but if you ever steal again, no trick in the world will be enough.'

The boy nodded frantically, promising never to let greed take over again. As they left the palace, Tenali pulled his nephew aside, whispering with a grin, 'Next time, if you want a golden apple, just ask. It's a lot easier than sneaking past an army of guards!'

The boy laughed nervously, but the lesson stayed with him, long after the sweet taste of apples had faded.

2

The Spy Astrologer's Betrayal

The Sultan of Bijapur was afraid.

His spies had brought troubling news. King Krishnadevaraya was preparing for war. If the Vijayanagara army crossed the Tungabhadra river, Bijapur would be crushed like a clay pot under an elephant's foot.

The sultan's army was weak. His resources were running thin. He needed a plan—one that didn't involve fighting.

One night, under the cover of darkness, he summoned his most trusted messenger. He placed a heavy pouch of gold coins in his hands.

'Take this,' the sultan ordered. 'Deliver it to Krishnadevaraya's royal astrologer. Tell him that he must convince the king at any cost not to go to war.'

The messenger rode through the night, his horse galloping like wildfire across the plains. By morning, the astrologer received the bribe, along with a sealed letter from the sultan.

His task was simple. Use fear; use fate. Just make sure the king never crosses the river. A few days later, the astrologer arrived at court. His forehead was creased with worry. His hands trembled just enough to look convincing.

He bowed before the king.

'My lord,' he whispered, his voice heavy with false concern, 'the stars ... they bring dark warnings. If you cross the Tungabhadra, disaster will befall you. Your life is at risk!'

The king frowned, rubbing his chin. He respected the wisdom of the stars. If danger lay ahead, perhaps it was wise to wait.

And so, he waited.

Days turned into weeks. Weeks turned into months. Every time the king felt the fire of war rising in his heart, the astrologer would arrive, sighing heavily and casting his eyes towards the heavens.

'The omens remain grim, my lord,' he would say. 'Delay the war for your own safety.'

Deep inside, a question gnawed at Krishnadevaraya. One evening, Krishnadevaraya summoned Tenali Raman to his chamber.

'Tenali,' the king said, his voice low with suspicion, 'the astrologer warns me against war, but I have my doubts.'

WHAT DO YOU THINK?
- ✤ Will Tenali outwit the astrologer?
- ✤ Can he find proof before it's too late?
- ✤ If you were in the court that day, what would you say to the king?

Tenali's sharp eyes glinted. 'Call him to court,' he said. 'Have him bring all his records. Let's see what the stars really say.'

The next morning, the royal court buzzed with whispers as the astrologer stood before the king, scrolls in hand. Once again, he repeated his warning.

'My lord,' he said, his voice firm, 'crossing the river spells doom. The stars do not lie.'

Tenali stepped forward, arms crossed. 'And what about your own stars, wise astrologer?' he asked, tilting his head. 'Tell me, do you foresee any danger to yourself?'

The astrologer scoffed. 'None at all,' he declared proudly. 'I have a long life ahead, one hundred years, at least.'

A slow smile spread across Tenali's face. 'Well then,' he said, 'let's test that prediction.'

With a snap of his fingers, he summoned the guards who had searched the astrologer's residence in his absence. They brought forward some scrolls and letters belonging to the astrologer. The court watched in stunned silence as the scrolls were unrolled. Letters, sealed with the mark of the sultan of Bijapur. Krishnadevaraya's expression darkened. He picked up one of the letters and read aloud: 'Stop the king from crossing the river by any means necessary.'

The room erupted in gasps. The astrologer fell to his knees, his face pale as moonlight.

'You betrayed your own king,' Tenali said, shaking his head. 'And you lied about your future. You claimed you would live a hundred years, but I fear you will not survive this day.'

Krishnadevaraya's voice was cold as steel. 'For treason, there is only one punishment.'

That evening, the astrologer met his fate. And the very next morning, King Krishnadevaraya rode across the Tungabhadra river leading his army to war. By nightfall, Bijapur had fallen. The sultan was defeated, and the war was won.

The stars cannot be bribed, and truth needs no horoscope. With the traitor gone and justice restored, the kingdom's courage returned, all because one man dared to question the heavens.

3

The Witness

In a quiet village, nestled among rolling green fields, lived a poor but honest man. For years, he had worked hard, saving every single penny he could. His dream? To go on a long pilgrimage.

As the day of his journey approached, he faced a worrying thought: what if bandits attacked him along the way? Carrying all his savings would be too risky. So, he decided to leave the money with someone he trusted. He approached a wealthy man from his village, known more for his riches than his warmth.

'Sir,' the poor man said, 'I will be away for a long time. Can you keep my money safe until I return?'

The rich man's eyes glinted for just a second before he put on a warm smile.

'Of course, my friend,' he said smoothly. 'I shall guard it like my own!'

But instead of handing over the money inside the house, the poor man did something ingenious. Right in front of the rich man, he dug a small pit beneath a large mango tree in the garden and buried the pouch of coins there. That way, there would be no confusion later. With a grateful heart, he set off on his journey.

Months passed.

The poor man returned home, his heart light with happiness, eager to reclaim his savings. He knocked on the rich man's door, smiling.

'Sir, I am back. Please return me my money.'

The rich man's smile vanished. His expression turned cold.

'Money?' he scoffed. 'I have never seen you before in my life! Why would a poor man like you even have such a large sum?'

The poor man's face fell. His hard-earned savings were gone!

IF YOU WERE IN HIS PLACE, HOW WOULD YOU RESPOND?
* Argue with the rich man?
* Gather the villagers for support?
* Or go to someone smart enough to outwit him?

The poor man was not one to give up easily. The next morning, the he arrived at the royal court of King Krishnadevaraya, pleading for justice. Tenali Raman, listening carefully, tapped his fingers on the table.

A knowing glint flashed in his eyes. 'Summon the rich man,' he said.

Soon, the wealthy trickster arrived at court, wearing an air of false innocence.

The king narrowed his eyes. 'Did you take this man's money?' he asked.

The rich man dramatically gasped. 'Me?' he cried, looking offended. 'I have never even seen this man before!'

Tenali leaned back. 'Oh, I see,' he said, stroking his chin. 'Well then … do you know what happens to liars in this court?'

The rich man swallowed hard but kept up his act. 'I don't know what you mean! If he claims he gave me money, where is the proof? Does he have a witness?'

Tenali smirked. 'Oh, but he does have a witness,' he said.

The court stilled. Even the king looked curious.

'The mango tree,' Tenali declared. 'The money was buried at its roots! The tree must have seen everything!'

The rich man's eyes darted around. 'The tree?' he scoffed. 'Are you saying a tree can talk?'

Tenali waved a hand dismissively. 'Of course! Even non-living things obey my magical powers.'

He turned to the poor man. 'Go to the garden,' Tenali instructed, 'and tell the mango tree that the king orders it to come to court and testify.'

The poor man hesitated. 'But ... a tree cannot walk, my lord.'

Tenali nodded gravely. 'True. But my magic is powerful. The tree will come on its own.'

The poor man obediently left the court. Time ticked by. An hour passed. Then, suddenly, Tenali turned to the rich man and asked casually, 'Why is the poor man taking so long? What could be delaying him?'

Without thinking, the rich man blurted out, 'Of course, he is taking time! The mango tree is more than six kilometres from here!'

The murmurs died down as once. All eyes turned towards the rich man. His face drained of colour. Tenali's smile widened. 'Aha,' he said softly, triumph flashing in his eyes. 'So you do know which mango tree we are talking about?'

The rich man froze. He had been caught! A slow chuckle escaped King Krishnadevaraya before it boomed into full laughter. 'The truth always finds its way, doesn't it?' he said.

The rich man, realising there was no escape, fell to his knees, ashamed and silent. 'I-I-I was tempted by greed, Your Majesty!' he stammered. 'Please forgive me!'

The king's face turned serious. 'Return the money to its rightful owner at once,' he commanded. 'Or you will face severe punishment!'

Shaking, the rich man reluctantly handed back every last coin. The poor man bowed to Tenali Raman. 'I am forever grateful for your wisdom, my lord.'

Tenali winked playfully. 'Next time,' he said, chuckling, 'let your witness be someone who can actually talk back!'

The courtroom erupted in laughter, and the dishonest rich man was imprisoned.

And the poor man? He would never forget the mango tree or the man who made it speak.

4

The Thorn That Told the Truth

A poor farmer worked from dawn to dusk, ploughing, sowing, harvesting, season after season. After years of toil, he managed to set aside a small fortune. It was all he had.

But where could he keep it safe?

The farmer had no locks, no chests, no guards. So, he did what many in his village had done before him, he buried his money under a tree.

It was safe there ... or so he thought.

One morning, his worst nightmare came true. The money was gone! Frantically, he dug deeper, searching for any trace of his savings. Nothing.

His hands trembled. His heart pounded. Who had stolen it? With no other option, he ran to the royal court of King

Krishnadevaraya, pleading for justice. The king, ever fair, listened carefully and ordered six suspects to be brought in for questioning. The guards searched their homes, their belongings and their clothes, but no money was found.

The ministers whispered among themselves. Some doubted the farmer's claim.

'Perhaps he lost the money himself,' one muttered.

'Maybe he never had it to begin with,' another said.

The farmer's face burned with humiliation. He knew the truth. But how could he prove it?

IF NO ONE BELIEVES YOUR TRUTH, HOW FAR WOULD YOU GO TO PROVE IT?
* Would you fight, plead?
* Or find a clever witness no one expects?

Finally, the king turned to the one man who always found the truth. Tenali Raman.

Tenali bowed before the king. 'Your Majesty, I request two days to investigate.'

The king nodded. 'Very well, Tenali. Find me the thief.'

Tenali did not waste time. He rode straight to the place where the farmer had buried his treasure. At first, the ground seemed normal. The tree stood tall, its roots deep in the earth. But then, something caught Tenali's eye. Scattered around the tree were tiny, spiky *gokhru* thorns.

A slow smile spread across Tenali's face. This was the clue he needed. He plucked a few thorns and returned to the palace. Two days later, the courtroom was packed. The six suspects stood in a line before the king. The farmer sat anxiously, hoping for justice.

Tenali stepped forward. His eyes gleamed with confidence. 'Your Majesty,' he said, 'I have found both the thief … and the witness.'

Gasps rippled through the court.

The king leaned forward. 'Who is the witness?'

Tenali smiled. 'The witness, Your Majesty, is not a who but a what. Bring the suspects forward.'

The six men stepped forward, looking nervous. Without asking any questions, Tenali knelt and examined their shoes. The room fell into a heavy silence.

After a moment, Tenali stood and pointed at one man. 'It's him.'

The suspect's face drained of colour. He opened his mouth to protest, but then he panicked.

'I confess!' he cried, dropping to his knees. It was me! 'I stole the money!'

The court erupted in shock.

The king turned to Tenali. 'How did you know?'

Tenali held up a small thorn. 'The money was buried under a tree covered with gokhru thorns,' he explained. 'Anyone who stepped near it would have these tiny thorns stuck in their shoes.'

He gestured to the guilty man. 'This suspect had the same thorns stuck in his soles. That was all the proof I needed.'

The thief hung his head in shame as the guards seized him.

The king smiled, turning to the farmer. 'Your savings will be returned at once.'

Tears of gratitude filled the farmer's eyes. 'Thank you, Your Majesty. And thank you, Tenali Raman!'

The court erupted in applause.

And once again, Tenali Raman had proven that wit is sharper than any sword. The thorn had spoken. And the truth was unburied in no time.

IF YOU WERE A DETECTIVE, HOW WOULD YOU FIND A THIEF WITH NO WITNESSES?

- Would you search for clues?
- Would you use logic and observation?
- Or would you, like Tenali, let the smallest detail lead you to the truth?

5

The Precious Box

The royal court of Vijayanagara was abuzz with activity. Ministers whispered, advisors debated and the golden throne gleamed under the morning sun. But amidst the serious discussions, one man walked in with a glint in his eyes. Tenali Raman.

And in his hands, he held a tiny box.

King Krishnadevaraya, noticing Tenali's smug expression, raised an eyebrow. 'Tenali, what is it this time?'

Without a word, Tenali stepped forward and placed the box on the king's palm. The entire court leaned in as the king slowly lifted the lid. Inside lay a gold box, encrusted with dazzling gems, a masterpiece, glittering like it belonged in the royal treasury itself.

The king's eyes widened in admiration. 'This is exquisite! Where did you find it?'

Tenali chuckled, tilting his head. 'That's the interesting part, Your Majesty. These boxes have been spreading like wildfire. And guess what? They are gifts.'

'Gifts?' The king frowned.

'Yes, Your Majesty. Gifts from a certain tax officer. A very generous man.'

The murmurs in the court grew louder. A tax officer? Handing out treasures? That didn't add up.

'Tell me, Tenali,' the king said, his expression growing serious, 'who is this officer?'

'Ah,' Tenali said, leaning in. 'That's the fun part. He's not just handing these out for charity. He's been giving them to your own ministers.'

There was a hush.

'Why?' the king demanded.

'Because, Your Majesty,' Tenali's voice dropped to a whisper, 'once a minister accepts such an extravagant gift, he will owe the officer a favour.'

'And what favour is that?'

'Simple,' Tenali shrugged. 'Whenever he raises taxes unfairly, they stay silent. After all, would they question the man who made them rich?'

The king's face darkened. His trusted advisors in his own court were being bought.

WHAT DO YOU THINK?
❖ If someone gave you a valuable gift, but you knew it came with strings attached, would you still accept it?

Krishnadevaraya clenched his fists. 'Guards! I want an immediate inquiry into every official who received one of these boxes!'

The guards rushed out, and within hours, the truth unravelled, just as Tenali had warned. The tax officer had been siphoning money, inflating taxes and distributing bribes to secure his power. Several ministers had accepted the gifts while the people suffered. Hundreds of families had been overtaxed, their gold stolen under false pretences.

The king's expression turned stone cold. 'Seize all the wealth he has stolen,' he ordered. 'Let the people of Vijayanagara get back what is rightfully theirs!'

As the guards left to carry out his orders, the king turned back to Tenali. 'How did you find out about this?'

Tenali smirked. 'Your Majesty, some treasures shine too brightly. But real gold? That's honesty.'

The king laughed and patted Tenali's shoulder. 'Indeed, Tenali. You have once again saved my kingdom.'

Just like that, Tenali had turned a tiny box into a lesson that no one in the court would forget.

6

The Not-So-Golden Box

One hot afternoon, a wealthy trader strolled into the royal court of Vijayanagara. His gold-embroidered silk robes shimmered, and he carried a large, heavy metal box.

'Your Majesty,' he said, bowing deeply, 'I am about to embark on a long pilgrimage. This box contains my ancestral wealth, those treasures passed down through generations. I beg you to keep it safe in the royal treasury until I return.'

The king nodded thoughtfully. 'A man's legacy is sacred. Very well, your box will be safe here.'

But the royal treasurer frowned. 'Your Majesty, the treasury is already full. There is no space for another box!'

The king turned to Tenali Raman, his most trusted advisor. 'Tenali, would you mind keeping it in your home until the trader returns?'

Tenali smiled. 'Of course, Your Majesty.' He took the box home. Weeks passed.

One day, the trader stormed into the palace, demanding, 'My box! I want it back immediately!'

Tenali lifted the box, then stopped, puzzled. It felt suspiciously light, nothing like what you'd expect from a box filled with gold. He frowned and set it down in front of the trader.

Then he turned and asked, 'Are you absolutely sure this is your ancestral treasure?'

'Of course it is!' the trader snapped. 'Now give it to me!'

Tenali turned to the king with a small bow. 'Your Majesty, we seem to have a ... situation.'

The king raised an eyebrow. 'What kind of situation?'

Tenali clasped his hands with mock gravity. 'It appears the trader's ancestors have made themselves quite at home in my house. They're guarding the box and refuse to let it go.'

A stunned silence fell over the court. The trader's face turned crimson. 'This is nonsense! He's lying!'

The king, intrigued, ordered everyone to Tenali's house. When they arrived, Tenali dramatically opened the box and ants scurried out in every direction! He dipped his hand inside, and pulled out a handful of sugar!

He smiled knowingly. 'If this pot really contained gold for all these years ... would there still be sugar in it? Would the ants have left even a speck behind?'

Gasps echoed.

Tenali turned to the king and shook his head.

'Your Majesty, this box never held gold or jewels—only sugar. The trader's plan was to falsely claim that his treasure had been lost while in my care, hoping you would compensate him with real gold for what was never here to begin with.'

The king's face darkened.

'You dared deceive the throne?' The words rang out like a blade unsheathed—cold, sharp, final.

The trader trembled. 'M-my lord, I-I-'

'Enough!' The king ordered the trader's arrest on the spot.

As the guards dragged the fraudulent trader away, Tenali bowed and smiled.

'True treasure, Your Majesty,' he said, 'is built on honesty. Everything else is just sugar to the ants.'

The king laughed heartily.

'And once again, Tenali Raman proves that wisdom is the greatest wealth of all.'

The court erupted in applause. The dishonest trader was caught by his own greed and a little sugar.

IF SOMEONE ASKED YOU TO GUARD THEIR LEGACY, HOW MIGHT YOU HANDLE IT?

* Would you trust them?
* Or check the truth yourself first?

7

The Head He Delivered Himself

One fateful day, Tenali Raman managed to anger King Krishnadevaraya, so much so that the king, in a fit of rage, ordered his execution.

The entire court fell silent. No one dared to argue.

But Tenali's wife, who was as sharp as her husband, whispered a brilliant idea to him before he was taken away.

WHAT WOULD YOU DO IF YOU WERE IN TENALI'S PLACE?
- Would you beg for mercy?
- Would you try to escape?
- Would you find a way to turn the situation in your favour?

When the royal guard arrived to take Tenali to the execution grounds, Tenali smiled calmly and said, 'I'll stay alive, don't worry.'

The guard, puzzled but fond of Tenali, asked, 'How?'

Tenali replied, 'What did the king tell you to do?'

'The king wanted us to bring your head.'

'Then don't worry, just take me back.' So, they escorted him back to the king's court the next day.

The moment Tenali walked in, the king's eyes flared with anger. 'How dare you disobey me?' he growled.

Tenali, completely unfazed said, 'Your Majesty, I never trust anyone else to handle important matters for me. 'My head is so precious, these fools may lose it.' Then, he grinned and added, 'So, I decided to bring my head to you myself.'

For a moment, the court was silent. Then, there was bellowing laughter! Even the king himself could not resist chuckling.

Krishnadevaraya shook his head, amused. 'Tenali, your wit is sharper than a sword. How can I punish a man who outsmarts me every time?'

With that, he forgave Tenali once again, amazed by his cleverness.

In a moment when swords and tempers flared, it was a woman's whisper that turned the tide.

'They wanted brawn,' Tenali told his wife later, 'but sometimes, brains do all the heavy lifting'.

His wife chuckled, 'Good thing our household has *two* brains doing the lifting!'

8

The Pot-faced Peacemaker

It was one of those days when Tenali Raman's sharp wit pushed King Krishnadevaraya a little too far. The court had been engaged in serious discussions, but Tenali, always the mischief-maker, had made a joke at the wrong time.

The king's face turned red with irritation. 'Enough, Tenali! Leave the court. I don't want to see your face again!'

The jealous courtiers, always looking for ways to get rid of Tenali, exchanged smirks as he exited the hall. But not long after, Tenali walked back into the courtroom.

WHAT WOULD YOU DO IF THE KING HAD JUST BANISHED YOU?
- ❖ Would you hide?
- ❖ Apologise?
- ❖ Or walk back in a clever way?

But this time, his face was completely covered with a large clay pot.

The king's anger flared up again. 'Tenali! Didn't I just say that I don't want to see your face?'

From inside the pot, Tenali's muffled voice replied, 'Indeed, Your Majesty. That is why I made sure you can't see my face.'

The king's brows furrowed in confusion. 'What do you mean, Tenali?'

Tenali lifted his head slightly, revealing that the pot had only three small holes: two for his eyes and one for his mouth.

'See, Your Majesty?' he said cheerfully. 'You are looking at a pot, not my face. I have obeyed your command perfectly.'

For a moment, there was silence. Then, laughter exploded across the hall! Ministers clapped their hands. Guards struggled to keep a straight face. Even the jealous courtiers couldn't help but chuckle at Tenali's ridiculous, yet brilliant, solution.

The king, caught between amusement and exasperation, shook his head. 'You trickster! You always find a way around my words.'

But his anger was gone. He laughed heartily and waved his hand. 'Fine, Tenali! You may stay.'

Tenali removed the pot and bowed dramatically. 'Ah, Your Majesty, it's a relief to breathe again. Clay pots are useful but not very comfortable.'

The court erupted in laughter once more, and just like that, Tenali Raman had turned the king's ire into another victory for wit.

Oops, You've Been Outwitted!

Tenali's toolkit:
quick wit, a smirk
and royal facepalms.

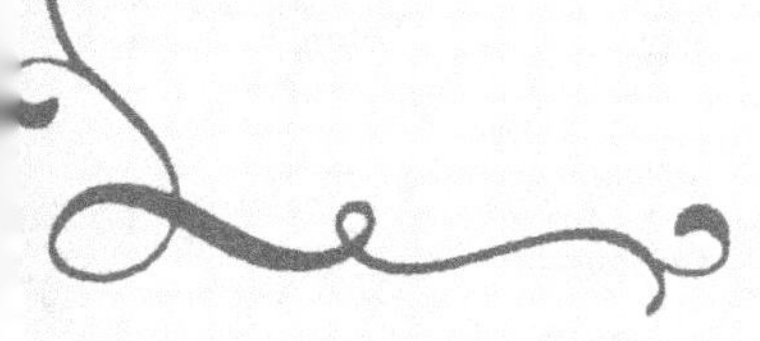

9

Tit for Tat

The town of Vijayanagara was alive with the sounds of cheerful chatter, drumbeats and ringing bells. The streets sparkled with festive decorations, and the scent of sweet jaggery and fresh flowers filled the air.

It was a special occasion—the sixtieth birthday of a beloved elderly Brahmin. The townspeople wanted to honour him with a grand procession through the city, seated atop a magnificent elephant.

But there was just one problem. They didn't own an elephant! So, they turned to Veerabhadra, a wealthy but notoriously quarrelsome merchant who owned the biggest elephant in town.

When the townspeople approached him with their request, Veerabhadra rubbed his chin. 'Hmm … I suppose you may borrow my elephant,' he said slyly.

The celebration went exactly as planned. Music played. Dancers twirled. Flowers rained from the balconies. It was a sight to behold.

By the end of the night, the townspeople, exhausted from all the merrymaking, decided to return the elephant first thing in the morning. But fate had other plans. When dawn arrived, so did bad news. The elephant had died in its sleep.

The moment Veerabhadra heard of his elephant's death, his face turned red. He stormed into the streets, his voice exploding like a thunderclap. 'You borrowed my elephant. Now return it!' he demanded.

The townspeople exchanged worried glances. 'But Sir, the elephant died a natural death,' one of them pleaded.

Another slightly affluent villager said, 'Perhaps we could compensate you for the elephant.'

Veerabhadra folded his arms. 'I don't want another elephant. I don't want money. I want you to return the same elephant. Alive!'

His ridiculous demand spread through the town like wildfire.

WHAT DO YOU THINK?
- ♣ If a man demands his dead elephant back, should you give him a live one?
- ♣ A statue?
- ♣ Or just a taste of his own nonsense?

Knowing they needed someone intelligent to handle the situation, the townspeople rushed to Tenali Raman. Tenali listened carefully. Then with mischief in his voice said, 'Ah, I have an idea.'

He whispered a plan to the townspeople. Then, turning to Veerabhadra, he said, 'Sir, I assure you that you will get your elephant back, but only if you agree to one condition.'

Veerabhadra squinted. 'What condition?'

'You must bring the leader of the town to the court tomorrow at exactly six in the morning. Do you agree?'

Eager to win his argument, Veerabhadra nodded instantly. 'Fine!' he snapped. 'I'll be there!'

The next morning, as the sun barely began to rise, Veerabhadra arrived at the leader's house. He knocked. No answer. He banged harder. Still no answer.

Annoyed, he slammed his fists against the door. And suddenly there was a loud crash!

A stack of earthen pots toppled over, shattering into a hundred pieces! Just then, the leader calmly stepped outside, pretending to be furious. 'You fool!' he shouted. 'You have destroyed my ancestral pots! How will I get them back now?'

Veerabhadra blinked in confusion. 'What? How can I return broken pots? That's impossible!'

The leader folded his arms. 'Ah,' he said, smiling slightly. 'So you understand that some things, once lost, cannot be returned?'

Later that morning, as they stood before the king, Veerabhadra turned to Tenali Raman. 'Now, where is my elephant?' he demanded.

Tenali feigned innocence. 'Sir, the townspeople are ready to return it, but first, you must return the leader's ancestral pots.'

The entire court went silent. Then, realisation hit. Veerabhadra's face turned beet red. He had walked straight into Tenali's trap!

Sometimes, the best reply to nonsense is more nonsense. With a pinch of wit. The courtroom, which had been tense with anticipation, suddenly erupted in laughter. Ministers chuckled, the king smirked and even the guards struggled to hide their amusement.

Tenali folded his hands respectfully and said, 'Sir, return his pots, and he will return your elephant.'

Veerabhadra grumbled, then sighed in defeat. 'Fine,' he muttered, throwing up his hands. 'I withdraw my demand!'

The townspeople cheered. As they walked away, Tenali leaned towards the leader and whispered, 'Next time, let's celebrate without an elephant.'

10

Rewriting the Mahabharata

The court of the Delhi Sultanate was a place of power, intrigue and grand displays of intellect. It was here that King Krishnadevaraya once found himself, seated among silk-draped pillars and golden chandeliers, invited as an honoured guest. But he quickly realised that this was no ordinary meeting. The sultan was known for his sharp mind and even sharper tests.

'Your Majesty,' he said, stroking his beard, 'I have always admired the great Mahabharata.'

Krishnadevaraya nodded cautiously.

The sultan continued, smiling slyly. 'I have just one simple request. Rewrite the epic. But this time, Draupadi should be married to the Kauravas, not the Pandavas.'

WHAT WOULD DO IF YOU WERE THE KING?
* ❖ Agree to rewrite it just to keep the peace?
* ❖ Refuse outright and risk offending the sultan?
* ❖ Or find a way to outwit him without conflict?

The king's breath caught in his throat. Was he hearing this correctly? There was pin-drop silence. Ministers glanced at each other, unsure whether to gasp or laugh. The Mahabharata was sacred. It was not some story to be changed at will!

And yet, refusing the sultan outright could insult him and lead to dangerous consequences. Krishnadevaraya's mind raced for a solution. But before he could respond, a voice broke the silence. A calm, confident voice.

Tenali Raman stepped forward and with amusement in his voice said, 'Your Majesty, allow me to handle this.'

Krishnadevaraya exhaled in relief. If anyone could find a way out of this royal trap, it was Tenali. The court watched in anticipation as Tenali turned to the sultan with a knowing smile.

'My lord,' Tenali began, 'rewriting the Mahabharata is no small feat. It is kind of like rewriting history to make sure your favourite team always wins the championship!'

The sultan's brows furrowed slightly.

'But,' Tenali continued, 'before I begin, I must make one small request of you.'

The sultan leaned forward curiously. 'And what is that?'

Tenali folded his hands politely. 'Your Majesty,' he said, 'before rewriting the Mahabharata, I must first rewrite history itself. You see, in order for the Kauravas to marry Draupadi, they must first win her hand at the swayamvar.'

The sultan nodded slowly. 'Yes…?'

'But history states that Arjuna won Draupadi by displaying exceptional skill. So before I can change the Mahabharata, I must first go back in time and change history.' He paused dramatically. 'Can you grant me the power to do so?'

The sultan's eyes widened. The court held its breath. And then the sultan could not hold back his hearty laugh. 'You are truly wise, Tenali Raman!' he declared. 'Now I see how foolish my request was!'

His hearty laughter filled the hall, and the tension in the air melted away. 'I withdraw my demand,' the sultan said, shaking his head. 'You have bested me with your famed wit.'

In a court full of astute men, Tenali played the game like a grandmaster, turning blasphemy into brilliance and leaving even sultans in checkmate with a smile.

11

Slaying with Sarcasm

The Tungabhadra river shimmered under the golden afternoon sun as King Krishnadevaraya and his royal entourage wandered far from the city, enjoying a peaceful outing. Birds chirped, the river breeze was cool and gentle, and for once, the king allowed himself to relax. But peace rarely lasts for long.

IF YOUR KING WAS AMBUSHED AND OUTNUMBERED, WHAT WOULD YOU DO?

* Pick up a sword?
* Run?
* Or try something wildly unexpected?

Just as the king's guards had let down their guard, the ground rumbled beneath the quake of galloping hooves. From behind the trees, a great dust cloud rose, and before anyone could react …

AMBUSH!

Swords clashed, arrows whizzed through the air and suddenly, the calm riverbank had turned into a battlefield. The attack was swift and ruthless.

Leading the charge was Pasara Govinda Raju, a ruthless warlord known for his cunningness and brutality. His soldiers surrounded the king's guards like a pack of hungry wolves. Krishnadevaraya's men fought bravely but they were soon outnumbered.

Just then, Tenali Raman's voice rang out utterly fearless. Instead of drawing a sword, Tenali stepped forward, his hands empty and his eyes glinting with mischief.

He faced Pasara Govinda Raju and smirked. 'Ah, the mighty Pasara Govinda Raju,' he called out, loud enough for everyone to hear.

The warlord paused, intrigued.

'Tell me,' Tenali continued, 'is it true that you were born to a donkey and raised by a goat?'

The battle froze for a second. Soldiers on both sides blinked in confusion. Govinda Raju's face twisted in rage. 'You dare insult me?' His voice struck like steel.

Tenali replied, 'Oh, my apologies! I was just wondering since your battle style looks less like a warrior's and more like a clumsy buffalo running in circles.'

The king's soldiers stifled chuckles.

Govinda Raju's fists clenched. 'HOW DARE YOU!'

'Oh, I dare, all right,' Tenali interrupted, still calm as ever. 'You see, my dear Pasara, true warriors fight with their minds, not just their swords. But you ... well, you seem more beast than man.'

That was the last straw.

Enraged beyond control, Govinda Raju lunged forward and in that blind moment of fury, he left himself wide open.

SLASH!

A swift stroke from a nearby soldier cut him down instantly. His body collapsed onto the dust. For a brief, frozen moment, the battlefield was silent.

Then, realisation dawned. Their leader was dead. The invincible Pasara Govinda Raju had been defeated with words. Fear overtook his army. Their strength vanished like mist in the sun. One by one, they dropped their weapons. Some ran for their lives, others surrendered.

The only sound left was the victorious cheer of Krishnadevaraya's soldiers. Breathing heavily but safely, the king turned to Tenali, awe in his eyes.

'You saved us all,' he said, shaking his head in amazement.

Tenali bowed playfully. 'Well, Your Majesty, I figured it was easier to kill his pride than to fight his army.'

Krishnadevaraya laughed heartily. 'You truly are a genius, Tenali!'

The court had never seen a battle won in such an unusual way.

'As a reward,' the king said playfully, 'I will grant you a wish.'

Tenali pretended to think hard. Then, with a twinkle in his eye, he said: 'Your Majesty, I request a pardon for a hundred sins I might commit in the future.'

The king raised an eyebrow. 'Only a hundred?'

Tenali sighed dramatically. 'Well, I was trying to be humble.'

The king roared with laughter. 'In that case, I shall pardon a thousand!'

The court erupted in cheers, and from that day forward, Tenali Raman was remembered as a master strategist.

12

The Painted Pigeon

The royal court of Vijayanagara was always filled with interesting visitors. Merchants, scholars, performers and travellers from faraway lands.

But on this particular morning, the palace gates opened for an unusual guest. A bird-catcher stepped forward, carrying a small golden cage. Inside it sat a bird unlike any seen before. Its feathers shimmered in dazzling shades of green, blue and crimson, glowing like precious jewels under the sunlight.

The courtiers gasped in admiration.

WHAT WOULD YOU DO IF YOU FOUND SUCH A RARE BIRD?
- ✤ Would you keep it as a treasure?
- ✤ Set it free?
- ✤ Or try to find out more about it?

The bird-catcher bowed deeply. 'Your Majesty, this is no ordinary bird. This is the rarest species in the world. A true marvel!'

King Krishnadevaraya's eyes gleamed with excitement. 'Indeed, it is magnificent,' he exclaimed. He reached for his gold pouch, ready to reward the man handsomely. But, just as he was about to place the gold coins in the bird-catcher's hands, a calm voice interrupted.

'Wait, Your Majesty.' All eyes turned towards Tenali Raman.

The bird-catcher frowned. 'Are you questioning my honesty, Tenali Raman?'

Tenali tilted his head slightly, his sharp eyes observing every detail. Then, he picked up a jug of water and walked towards the cage. Without another word, he poured the water gently over the bird.

The courtiers gasped. The bright colours began to drip away! The shimmering bird transformed into an ordinary pigeon. The grand illusion was gone. The king stared, stunned. Even the golden cage looked duller now.

Finally, he turned to Tenali. 'How did you know?'

Tenali smiled. 'It was simple, Your Majesty. I noticed the bird-catcher's fingernails.'

The courtiers leaned in, curious.

'They were stained with the same bright colours. He had painted the pigeon to trick you.'

A wave of whispers spread across the court. The king's astonishment quickly turned to anger. 'Guards! Seize this trickster at once!'

The bird-catcher fell to his knees, trembling. 'Forgive me, Your Majesty! I was only trying to earn a few gold coins. I meant no harm!'

The king frowned. 'You had a chance to earn your reward with truth. But you chose to lie and almost fooled an entire court.'

The bird-catcher looked down, ashamed.

WHAT DO YOU THINK SHOULD BE HIS PUNISHMENT?

♣ A fine?

♣ A lesson in honesty?

♣ Or perhaps a chance to make things right?

The king paused, then raised a hand. 'Wait.'

He turned to Tenali. 'What do you think we should do with him?'

Tenali considered for a moment, then said, 'Let him paint walls in the palace instead. If he must use colours, let it be for beauty, not deceit. But let him also sweep the bird cages and learn that no job is too small when done honestly.'

The court murmured in approval.

The king smiled. 'Very well. You will work under royal watch. Perhaps truth will teach you what trickery could not.'

The bird-catcher had narrowly escaped punishment. As the court settled down, Krishnadevaraya turned to Tenali, 'Once again, you have saved me from his deception.'

Tenali chuckled. 'Your Majesty, beauty is not always what it seems. Sometimes, all it takes is a little water to wash away the lies.'

The king laughed, nodding in agreement.

'And sometimes,' Tenali added with a smile, 'a second chance is the best colour we can offer someone who has lost their way.'

13

The Clever Choice of Death

The kingdom of Vijayanagara was thriving, and that made the sultan of Bijapur uneasy.

King Krishnadevaraya was strong, wise and loved by his people. If left unchecked, he would soon become the most powerful ruler in the land.

The sultan knew he had to act fast. But how do you defeat a king who is always a step ahead? By turning his most trusted advisor against him.

The sultan found the perfect pawn—Kanakaraju, a greedy courtier who had once been a friend of Tenali Raman. For a bag of gold, Kanakaraju agreed to frame Tenali and remove him from the king's favour forever.

He hired an assassin and forged a letter in Tenali's handwriting. The letter invited the king to a lonely forest clearing under the pretence of discussing an urgent matter. And there, in the shadows, the assassin waited.

IF YOU RECEIVED A LETTER FROM YOUR MOST TRUSTED ADVISOR, ASKING YOU TO MEET IN SECRET, WHAT WOULD YOU DO?
* Would you risk going alone?
* Would you take guards?
* Or would you pause to wonder if something was amiss?

King Krishnadevaraya, always confident in his strength, rode out alone. But the moment he arrived, a dagger flashed through the air. The assassin struck!

The king, trained in battle, dodged just in time. A fierce fight followed. But the assassin was no match for a warrior king. Within minutes, he was captured. Under threat of punishment, the assassin revealed everything. Krishnadevaraya's anger flared. Tenali Raman had betrayed him?

The next morning, the king stormed into court. His face was like a thundercloud. 'Summon Tenali!' he ordered.

Tenali entered, puzzled by the king's fury.

'I trusted you,' Krishnadevaraya said, his voice dangerously calm. 'And you betrayed me?'

Tenali's eyes widened. 'Your Majesty, I swear on my life, I would never…'

But the king had already decided. 'If you truly are innocent, let fate decide. But I shall punish you with death. Since I am merciful, you may choose how.'

IF YOU WERE TENALI, WHAT WOULD YOU SAY?
* Would you beg for mercy?
* Try to explain?
* Or come up with a clever trick?

An eerie silence fell, so complete that even the court banners forgot to flutter. Ministers held their breath. The guards exchanged uneasy glances. Then Tenali said something totally unexpected.

He clasped his hands together, bowed respectfully and said, 'Your Majesty, I humbly request the greatest mercy. Let me die … of old age.'

For a moment, there was silence. Then laughter rippled across the entire court!

Krishnadevaraya, who had been furious just moments ago, threw back his head and laughed so hard that the royal guards nearly dropped their spears.

'You cunning fox!' the king gasped between laughs. 'You've wriggled out of this one too!'

By now, the king had calmed down enough to think clearly. He ordered an investigation. Soon, Kanakaraju's forgery was exposed. The treacherous courtier was caught red-handed and thrown out of the kingdom.

And as for Tenali?

Krishnadevaraya shook his head, still chuckling. 'You have a talent for escaping trouble, my friend.'

Tenali grinned. 'And you, my king, have a talent for keeping things interesting!'

WHAT DO YOU THINK?
* Can humour be a shield when logic fails?
* Could laughter be your last defence?

Whatever the answer, one thing was certain. Tenali Raman always found a way to win—through his unmatched wit.

14

The Best Artist

King Krishnadevaraya sat on his throne, deep in thought. His beloved uncle had passed away, and he wished to honour him with a grand portrait.

But there was a problem.

The beloved uncle had been blind in one eye, and the king was determined that the painting should be both truthful and respectful. He summoned three of the greatest artists in the kingdom and set a challenge.

'Paint my uncle's portrait. If it is good, you will be rewarded. But if you fail, you will be punished.' The artists trembled. It was a dangerous task.

WHAT WOULD YOU DO IN THEIR PLACE?
- ✤ Would you paint him as he truly was?
- ✤ Or try to please the king?

The first artist thought long and hard. Honesty is best, he decided. He painted the uncle exactly as he had been in life, with one eye shut.

The moment the king saw it, his face darkened. 'How dare you insult my uncle?' he shouted, voice shaking with rage.

The artist pleaded for mercy, but the king was furious. 'You have made him look weak. Guards! Punish him!'

The poor artist was thrown out of the court.

The second artist took a different approach. 'I will flatter the king,' he thought.

He painted the prince with two bright, perfect eyes. The moment the king saw it, his rage returned. 'Lies! My uncle was never like this!'

The second artist was punished even more intensely than the first.

The third artist, watching from the side, began sweating. He knew he was in trouble.

That night, he snuck into the palace gardens to seek help from the one man who could solve any problem—Tenali Raman. 'Tenali, help me! How do I paint the prince without making the king angry?'

Tenali smirked. 'Ah, this is simple. Listen carefully...'

The next morning, the artist stood before the king, calm and confident. He unveiled his painting.

The court gasped.

The king's expression softened.

The painting showed the prince in profile, turned slightly to one side, with only his good eye visible. It was truthful, yet respectful.

The king nodded. 'This is perfect. You have captured his dignity and strength.'

The artist was rewarded with gold and royal honours. As the court cheered, the artist turned to Tenali and winked. Once again, Tenali's wisdom had turned danger into victory.

Sometimes true art lies in what's left unsaid.

15

The Demon's Share

One evening, as Tenali Raman walked through his fields, a terrifying voice rumbled behind him.

'Mortal! These lands belonged to my ancestors. From now on, I demand half of whatever you grow here!'

Tenali turned to see a giant demon with glowing red eyes and smoke curling from his nostrils. Most men would have run for their lives. But not Tenali.

WHAT WOULD YOU DO IN TENALI'S PLACE?
* Would you refuse and risk angering the demon?
* Or would you find a smart way to outwit him?

He folded his hands respectfully and said, 'Of course. It is only fair that you take your share.'

The demon smirked, pleased.

Tenali stroked his chin and said, 'This year, take whatever grows above the ground.'

The demon grinned. 'Agreed!'

Months passed, and the demon returned for his harvest. But when he arrived, he roared in fury. 'What is this? You tricked me!'

The field was filled with potatoes. The demon had claimed everything above the ground, but potatoes grow underground. All he got was a pile of worthless leaves and stems.

Meanwhile, Tenali enjoyed a delicious feast of potatoes! The demon's face burned with anger.

IF YOU WERE THE DEMON, WHAT WOULD YOU DO NEXT?

♣ Would you take revenge?

♣ Or would you change the deal?

The demon gritted his teeth. 'Fine! Next time, I will take everything that grows underground!'

Tenali nodded politely. 'As you wish.'

Months later, the demon returned again. This time, he was certain he had won. But when he saw the field, his jaw dropped. The land was covered with golden corn!

The demon had claimed everything underground, but corn grows above the soil.

This time he was left with nothing but useless roots!

Furious and humiliated, the demon let out a howl of defeat. 'You tricked me again! This land is cursed! I will never return!'

And with that, he vanished into the mist. Tenali sat back, grinning. He had not fought the demon with weapons. He had not argued with the demon in anger.

Instead, he had used something far more powerful. His intelligence!

16

The Three Pots

As a wealthy landowner lay on his deathbed, his sons gathered around him, waiting for his final words. 'My dear sons,' he whispered weakly, 'after I am gone, dig under my bed. There, you will find my final gift to you.'

And with that, he took his last breath.

Days later, the brothers did as he had instructed. With eager hands, they dug into the earth, hoping to uncover gold, jewels or hidden treasures. Instead, they found three clay pots.

The first was filled with mud.

The second contained cow dung.

The third was stuffed with straw.

The brothers stared at their so-called inheritance, bewildered.

WHAT WOULD YOU DO IN THEIR PLACE?
- ♣ Would you assume it was a joke?
- ♣ Would you throw the pots away in frustration?
- ♣ Or would you seek someone wise enough to unravel the mystery?

Not knowing what else to do, the brothers turned to Tenali Raman.

Tenali examined the pots carefully, rubbing his chin. Then, he smiled. 'Your father was a wise man,' he said. 'He has already divided the inheritance among you.'

The brothers leaned in eagerly. 'The mud in the first pot represents land. The eldest son inherits the fields.'

The eldest nodded in understanding. 'The cow dung in the second pot symbolizes cattle. The second son gets the livestock.'

The second son sighed in relief.

'And the straw, golden in colour, represents wealth. The youngest son gets the riches.'

The brothers smiled, satisfied that their father had indeed left them something valuable.

But just as they were about to leave, the youngest noticed something glinting at the bottom of his pot. 'A silver coin!' he exclaimed. 'What does this mean, Tenali?'

Tenali chuckled, pocketing the coin with a wink. 'That,' he said, 'is my fee for solving the riddle!'

The brothers laughed, realising that even in matters of wisdom, Tenali never missed an opportunity.

Riddle Me This, Raja!

Where questions
are curiouser,
and answers curiouser still.

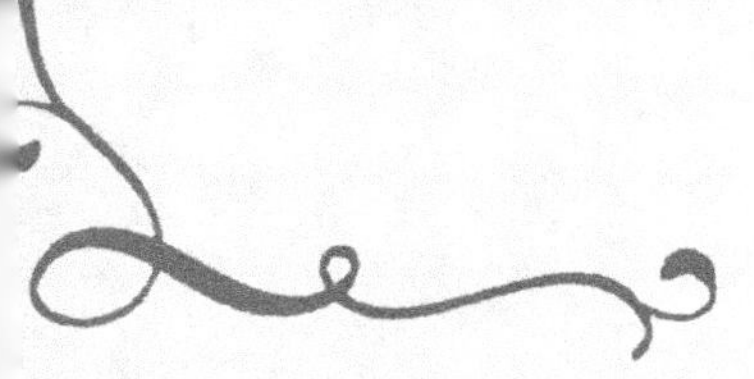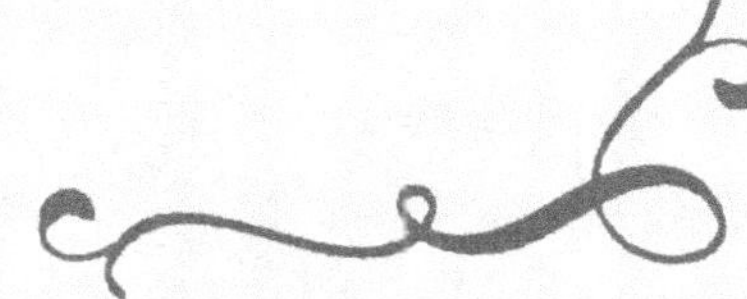

17

Truth and Lie

The grand court of Vijayanagara was buzzing with excitement. Scholars, philosophers and ministers sat in deep discussion, their robes flowing like river currents, their minds sharp as blades. King Krishnadevaraya, seated on his golden throne, leaned forward and with curiosity declared, 'I have a question for you all!'

The court silently awaited his words.

WHAT DO YOU THINK THE KING WILL ASK?
* A question about war?
* A riddle about wealth?
* Or something completely unexpected?

The king's voice echoed through the chamber. 'What is the difference between truth and a lie?'

A murmur spread across the court. The scholars stroked their beards, some tapping their chins thoughtfully.

Then, one wise old scholar stood up and declared, 'Your Majesty, the meaning of truth is entirely different from that of a lie!'

Another nodded in agreement. 'It is like the vast distance between the sky and the earth,' he added grandly.

The king nodded thoughtfully, but his curiosity remained unsatisfied. He turned to Tenali Raman, who had been listening silently, his arms crossed and a mischievous smile playing on his lips. 'Tenali, what do you think?' the king asked.

Tenali chuckled. 'Oh, King!' he said, shaking his head. 'I don't believe the difference is as great as the scholars say.'

The court stiffened in surprise. 'You don't?' the king asked, raising an eyebrow.

'Actually,' Tenali said, 'the difference between truth and a lie is much smaller than we think.'

The court fell into an uneasy silence. The scholars frowned, some whispering, 'What nonsense is this?'

The king leaned forward, intrigued. 'How small?'

Tenali grinned. 'The difference between truth and a lie,' he said, 'is just the distance between the eye and the ear!'

A few ministers gasped. The king's brows furrowed in curiosity. 'Explain,' he ordered.

Tenali spread his arms dramatically. 'What the eyes see is truth. What the ears hear is a lie. That's how small the difference is!'

For a moment, the court was silent. Then laughter erupted! Scholars nodded in admiration. Ministers clapped in appreciation. The king's laughter rang out, clear and full.

Krishnadevaraya rose from his throne, beaming. 'Tenali, what you have said is indeed correct!' he declared, embracing him warmly.

'Once again, you have shown that wisdom is not about lengthening words, but sharpening them!'

The court cheered, and Tenali bowed with a knowing smile.

Then the king turned to the court and said, 'Let us remember this always: don't believe everything you hear. See it for yourself if you want to know the truth.'

And from that day onwards, whenever someone in Vijayanagara tried to spread rumours or lies, they were reminded: 'The difference between truth and a lie is only the distance between the eye and the ear!'

18

Can a Black Dog Become White?

The grand kingdom of Vijayanagara was filled with splendid palaces, bustling markets and wise scholars. One day, something unusual happened. Tenali was missing at court.

The king sat impatiently on his throne, tapping his fingers against the armrest. 'Where is Tenali?' he demanded, his voice echoing through the court.

The guards scrambled to find him, and soon enough, Tenali hurried in, bowing deeply.

The king's eyebrows furrowed. 'You are late,' he said sternly. 'Why?'

Tenali sighed dramatically, as if he had just returned from a great battle. 'Forgive me, Your Majesty,' he said. 'I was performing a very special ritual.'

The king raised an eyebrow. 'A ritual?'

'Yes, my lord,' Tenali said, nodding solemnly. 'I have been trying to turn a black dog into a white one.'

The courtroom quieted as if holding its breath. Ministers exchanged confused glances.

One guard whispered to another, 'Did he say ... he's trying to change a dog's colour?'

The king, now curious, leaned forward. 'And how exactly do you plan to do that?' he asked.

Tenali sighed again, as if he were carrying the burden of a great secret. 'By bathing the dog every day, applying sacred oils and reciting powerful mantras, I hope to change its colour,' he declared.

The king stared at him for a moment. And then laughed with mirth! The entire court burst into laughter as well.

The king wiped tears from his eyes. 'You fool!' he chuckled. 'No matter how many times you bathe a black dog, it will always remain black!'

The ministers and guards nodded in agreement, still grinning at the absurdity of the idea.

WHAT DO YOU THINK?

* Is Tenali truly foolish, or is he trying to teach the king a lesson?
* Could there be a deeper meaning behind his strange 'ritual'?

Just then, Tenali smiled knowingly. 'Exactly, my lord,' he said.

The king's laughter faded. The court grew silent again.

'And yet, every day,' he continued, 'you surround yourself with men who are wicked at heart, hoping that their nature will change.'

The king's expression hardened.

'Can an evil man ever become good just because he stands near goodness?' Tenali asked.

The king thought deeply. He glanced at his ministers, his guards and the courtiers surrounding him. How many among them were truly loyal? How many were just flatterers, pretending to be faithful while working for their own gain?

The lesson had hit its mark.

The king nodded slowly, his amusement replaced by wisdom. 'You have opened my eyes today,' he said, looking at Tenali with newfound respect.

From that day on, King Krishnadevaraya paid closer attention to the people around him. He ensured that his court was filled with honest men, not just those who flattered him.

And as for Tenali?

He gave up trying to change black dogs, but thanks to him, a few wolves in the court stopped pretending to be lambs.

19

I Am Always Empty

One morning, something unusual happened in the grand court of Vijayanagara.

Tenali Raman, who was usually full of energy, mischief and laughter, sat silently in a corner. He wasn't cracking jokes. He wasn't playing tricks. He wasn't even smiling. Instead, he looked pale, serious and deeply troubled.

King Krishnadevaraya, who knew Tenali as the court's brightest spark, immediately noticed the change. 'Tenali,' he asked gently, 'you look dull today. Is something wrong?'

Tenali sighed deeply and rose to his feet. 'Maharaja, how can I explain?' he said, his voice unusually low. 'An astrologer has given me terrible news.'

He paused. Everyone leaned in. 'He told me that I will die in two months.'

Ministers whispered nervously. Some gasped. Others scoffed.

But the king burst into laughter. 'You believe that nonsense, Tenali? You? Of all people?'

Tenali didn't smile. 'Your Majesty, death is not nonsense. It is the one thing that no one escapes.'

'But I'm not worried for myself,' he continued. 'It's my family I'm worried about. My wife and children, how will they survive without me?'

The court quieted again. Some ministers looked uneasy.

The king chuckled softly. 'Oh, Tenali. Don't let fear fool you. Life and death are beyond our control. There's no point wasting your days in worry.'

Tenali stared at him for a long moment. And then, suddenly, he smiled, his usual grin sneaking back onto his face. 'Aha! My lord! You are right, as always!' he said, bowing low. 'If I die, you will surely take care of my family. Won't you?'

The king's smile froze. The court erupted in laughter. He had walked right into Tenali's trap. 'You tricked me into promising that!' the king said, shaking his head.

Tenali bowed again. 'I am always empty, my lord, except when I am full of wit!'

The court laughed out loud. The next day, Tenali didn't come to the palace.

The king noticed. 'Perhaps he's taken the day off,' he said casually.

But then came a second day … and a third. Now the king grew concerned. He sent a messenger to check on Tenali.

The messenger returned, breathless. 'Tenali Raman is sick with fever!' he announced. 'He lies in bed, barely able to speak.'

The court gasped. The next day, the messenger returned again. This time, he looked pale. 'Tenali Raman is unconscious, Your Majesty!'

The king stood up, alarmed. 'This is serious.'

And then, on the third day, came the worst news of all.

The messenger burst into court, shouting, 'Your Majesty! Bad news!'

The court held its breath.

'Ramakrishna is no more!' the messenger cried. 'His family just returned from the cremation ground.'

The king froze in shock.

'Tenali… is DEAD!'

Ministers dropped their fans. The queen herself sent a word of condolence. The king stood in silence, too stunned to speak.

After a long pause, he turned to his guards. 'Go to his house. Bring all his jewels, cash and valuables to the palace. His wife cannot protect them alone, they'll be safer in our treasury.'

The guards nodded and left immediately. Soon, they returned with a heavy wooden chest from Tenali's home.

The king examined it, running his hand along the polished lid. 'He never told me he had so much wealth,' he murmured. 'Break it open.'

A servant lifted a hammer. CRACK!

The box split open. And out sprang, Tenali Raman!

'Victory to Maharaja!' he shouted, throwing his arms wide. 'May the King of Vijayanagara live long!'

The king leapt back in shock. 'Ramakrishna? You're alive!'

Tenali asked with amusement, 'Who told you I was dead, Your Majesty?'

'You tricked the entire court!' the king exclaimed.

Tenali bowed. 'My lord, I merely followed your advice. You said not to fear death. I took your words seriously, so seriously, that, in fact, I decided to test how the world would react.'

The king narrowed his eyes. 'But what about the chest? The treasures?'

Tenali raised a finger. 'Ah! That, my king, is the greatest illusion of all.'

He opened the chest wider, revealing nothing but empty space. 'I am always empty, my lord, just like this box.'

The king frowned. 'But the gold and jewels I've given you over the years?'

'Gone!' Tenali said proudly. 'Donated to the poor, to scholars, to temples. I never kept anything. Not even a coin.'

An uneasy stillness spread through the court. And then, the king laughed. He laughed so hard that he had to wipe tears from his eyes.

'You tricked me … and taught me,' he said. 'You may be empty of gold, Tenali, but you are full of wisdom, full of loyalty and full of heart.'

He turned to the court. 'Let it be known, this man is richer than all of us combined.'

The court cheered.

WHAT WOULD YOU DO?
* If you had to prove your worth to the world, would you show your bank account?
* Or your bravery?
* Would you fill a chest with treasure?
* Or fill the world around you with laughter, goodness and cleverness, like Tenali?

20

Heaven on Earth

One afternoon, King Krishnadevaraya sat on his ornate throne, gazing at the golden pillars of his court. But something was missing, his usual radiant smile.

The royal advisors noticed his deep sighs and whispered among themselves.

Finally, the king spoke up. 'When I was a boy, I heard of a place so beautiful that people called it heaven on earth. I have always wanted to see such a place. Can any of you tell me where it is?'

Ministers glanced at one another, unsure how to respond. Some muttered guesses, perhaps in the Himalayas? Maybe in a hidden valley? But no one had a clear answer.

Then, from the corner of the hall, Tenali Raman stepped forward. 'Your Majesty, I know where it is!'

The king's face lit up. 'You do? Where?'

'That, my king, is a secret! But I can take you there.'

The ministers leaned forward, intrigued.

'However, to find it,' Tenali continued, 'I will need ten thousand gold coins and some time to travel.'

The king, eager to witness this paradise, nodded immediately. 'Go forth, Tenali! Find this heaven on earth and take me there!'

And with that, Tenali left on his journey.

Days passed.

Weeks passed.

The king, growing impatient, called for his ministers. 'Has anyone heard from Tenali?'

'Not yet, Your Majesty,' a minister replied hesitantly.

Finally one day Tenali returned to the court. 'Tenali, have you found heaven on earth yet?' the king asked.

Tenali smiled mysteriously. 'Just a few more days, Your Majesty, and I will take you there.'

Finally, Tenali stood before the king with confidence. 'Your Majesty, the moment has arrived! Tomorrow, we leave for heaven on earth.'

The king and his royal entourage set out the next morning, following Tenali with great anticipation.

WHERE DO YOU THINK TENALI WAS TAKING THEM?
* A hidden palace full of gold?
* A mystical valley covered in rare flowers?
* A secret kingdom in the clouds?

After hours of travel, Tenali led them to a lush green clearing. Towering trees stretched into the sky, their leaves dancing in the breeze. Vibrant flowers bloomed in every direction, filling the air with sweet fragrance. A crystal-clear river flowed nearby, reflecting the golden sun.

'Your Majesty, welcome to heaven on earth.'

The king and his ministers looked around, confused. 'Tenali, this is just a forest,' one of them muttered.

'Wait and watch,' Tenali whispered.

A gentle wind blew, rustling the trees. Then, all of a sudden there was rain. The drizzle turned into a refreshing shower, making the trees glisten like emeralds. The king stood still, feeling the cool raindrops on his skin. Then, as suddenly as it had begun, the rain stopped. The sun broke through the clouds.

A stunning rainbow stretched across the sky. At that moment, the king felt something strange.

'This ... this is beautiful.'

'This feels like a dream.'

Tenali smiled knowingly. 'And now, Your Majesty, let's taste what heaven offers.'

Villagers from a nearby farm arrived, carrying baskets of golden mangoes.

'Fresh from the trees, Your Majesty,' Tenali said, offering the king a slice.

The moment the king took a bite, his eyes widened.

'This is the sweetest mango I have ever tasted.'

The ministers, too, took a bite, and their faces lit up in delight. 'Indeed, this is heaven!'

The king took a deep breath, looking at the rainbow, the trees and the river. 'Tell me, Tenali,' he said, 'how far is this place from our kingdom?'

Tenali grinned. 'Your Majesty, not far at all. You are standing in it.'

The king looked around. The freshly washed trees, vibrant flowers, soft grass, cool breeze and juicy mangoes all around. Then, curiosity struck him.

'But Tenali, what did you do with the ten thousand gold coins I gave you?'

Tenali bowed with a smile. 'Your Majesty, I used the gold to buy the best seeds and plant trees across our kingdom.'

'With more greenery, Vijayanagara can truly be heaven on earth for generations to come.'

The king was deeply moved. 'You are right, Tenali! Our kingdom shall flourish because of your wisdom!'

And from that day onwards, the king ensured that more trees were planted, so that Vijayanagara would always remain a green paradise.

21

The Tiny Black Box

A strange rumour had spread through the peaceful kingdom of Vijayanagara.

A mysterious sage, Tribhangi Baba, had taken residence under an ancient banyan tree on the outskirts of the city. People whispered about him in hushed voices.

'They say he can fulfil any wish.'

'He knows secrets no one else does.'

'He has powers beyond imagination.'

And so, one by one, the people flocked to him, eager to test his miracles. But then came a shocking announcement.

The sage proclaimed loudly, 'Someone close to the king is plotting to dethrone him!'

The news reached the palace like wildfire. King Krishnadevaraya, troubled and suspicious, decided he must meet this mystical sage himself.

WHAT WOULD YOU DO IF YOU WERE THE KING?
* Would you trust the sage's words?
* Would you demand proof?
* Or would you call upon someone truly wise to uncover the truth?

The next morning, the king rode out with his guards, ministers, and of course, Tenali Raman. As soon as they arrived, Tribhangi Baba's piercing eyes locked onto the king.

He leaned forward, his voice deep and foreboding. 'Your Majesty,' he said, 'be careful! The one who wants to overthrow you is standing right beside you.'

The king's face paled. His heart pounded. 'Who?' he demanded. 'Tell me!'

The sage slowly pulled out a tiny black box from his robe. 'I have meditated for twelve years,' he declared, 'to capture the very essence of your enemy inside this box. Open it, and you will see their face.'

The king's hand hovered over the lid, his fingers trembling. But then, the sage held up a pouch of sacred ash.

'Before you open it,' he said, his voice commanding, 'apply this sacred ash on your forehead. Only then will the box reveal the truth.'

The tension in the air was thick. The ministers leaned forward, eager to see what would happen next. The king reached for the ash.

But before he could touch it, a voice rang out. 'Wait, Your Majesty!'

All eyes turned to Tenali Raman. He stepped forward, his arms crossed, his eyes wickedly amused.

'Before our king applies anything to his skin,' Tenali said, 'shouldn't we first see how sacred this ash truly is?'

The court murmured. The king hesitated. Tenali held the pouch aloft. 'If this ash is harmless and holy, then surely the sage wouldn't mind applying a little to his own forehead?'

The sage's eyes widened. His hands trembled.

'Well?' Tenali asked, voice calm but firm. 'Show us that it's safe.'

For a heartbeat, everything was still. Then, the sage turned and bolted.

'Seize him,' the king roared.

The guards lunged forward, catching the man before he could escape. Tenali calmly walked over, opened the pouch, dipped his finger inside and sniffed.

Then, he turned to the king and said four chilling words. 'This is deadly poison.'

A gasp rippled through the crowd.

'If you had applied this so-called sacred ash, Your Majesty,' Tenali said gravely, 'it would have been the end of you.'

The sage, who was no sage at all, was actually a spy, a traitor sent to assassinate the king under the guise of a holy man. As he was dragged away, the tiny black box was opened at last. Inside, there was nothing but emptiness.

The king turned to Tenali, his voice full of gratitude. 'Once again, Tenali Raman, your wit has saved the day.'

The court erupted in applause.

And as for the final lesson?

Sometimes, the real danger isn't in what's inside the box, it is the person handing it to you. The box remained silent, but the court echoed with laughter.

For once, silence had spoken louder than magic.

22

Eating Is an Illusion

The grand court of Vijayanagara was filled with the scent of incense, the murmur of scholars and the rustle of silk robes. King Krishnadevaraya sat on his throne, listening to a scholar delivering a deep and philosophical lecture.

'Everything in this world is an illusion,' the scholar declared. 'Nothing is real. Everything changes. Nothing truly belongs to us.'

The ministers nodded in approval. Some even closed their eyes, as if soaking in the divine wisdom. But in the corner of the room, Tenali Raman raised an eyebrow.

After a moment, he spoke up. 'Respected scholar, if everything is an illusion … what about eating? Surely food is real?'

The scholar scoffed, waving a dismissive hand. 'Foolish question! Eating is an illusion too! One moment, food is on the plate. The next moment, it has changed place! You think you are eating, but it is all *maya*, just an illusion.'

The king was delighted. 'Wonderful! What profound wisdom!' He bowed to the scholar and sought his blessings.

Tenali nodded, stroking his chin. 'Fascinating,' he murmured.

And then, he hatched a plan.

The next day, Tenali approached the scholar with a warm smile. 'Sir,' he said, 'your wisdom is unmatched. I would be honoured to host a grand banquet in your honour. Please come to my house tomorrow!'

The scholar, pleased, accepted the invitation. The next evening, he arrived at Tenali's home. The aroma of spices and ghee filled the air as guests began to arrive.

Servants rushed in and began serving food to everyone— everyone but the scholar.

He waited.

And waited.

Plates were refilled. Curries, idlis and sweets were served to everyone but him. His stomach rumbled. His fingers twitched. He watched helplessly as others enjoyed the feast.

Finally, when the last guest had finished and left, the scholar could take it no more.

He slammed his hand on the table. 'Ramakrishna! Where is my food?'

Tenali smiled calmly. 'Oh, food? But, my dear scholar, I thought you said eating was an illusion!'

The scholar's face turned red. 'Are you mocking me?' he spat out.

'Not at all!' Tenali said, his eyes twinkling.

The scholar fumed with rage. 'This is an insult,' he shouted, storming out of the house.

The next morning, he went straight to the palace, and cried, 'Tenali Raman insulted me, Your Majesty! I was humiliated!'

The king frowned and summoned Tenali. 'Tenali,' he said, 'why did you disrespect a great scholar?'

Tenali bowed. 'Your Majesty, I would never insult such wisdom. I simply followed his teachings. He himself said eating was an illusion, so I ensured that his meal also remained ... an illusion!'

For a moment, the court was silent. Krishnadevaraya's shoulders shook as laughter took over. The ministers chuckled. Even the scholar, after a moment, realised he had been trapped by his own words. The king wiped away tears of laughter and clapped Tenali on the shoulder.

'Tenali, only you can teach such a lesson in such a clever way!'

Tenali bowed with joy. And, that is how the man who turned philosophy into a joke and jokes into wisdom became the king's most trusted advisor.

WHAT ABOUT YOU?

* If someone told you that everything was an illusion, would you believe them?

* Or would you, like Tenali, put their words to the test?

23

True Beauty

King Krishnadevaraya sat on his golden throne, surveying his vast and powerful kingdom. His heart swelled with pride but something stirred within him, an ambition beyond war and wealth.

'I want Vijayanagara to be the most beautiful city in the world,' he declared. 'Let it be so grand that travellers call it a paradise on earth.'

His ministers nodded, and he turned to his most trusted official, Jai Singh, master of the city's design and order. 'You will oversee this task,' the king commanded. 'No expense shall be spared.'

Under Jai Singh's leadership, painters, sculptors and architects worked day and night. Grand palaces were polished until they glittered like gold. Lush gardens bloomed with rare flowers from across the kingdom. Fountains danced under the sunlight, filling the air with mist. The streets were paved in white stone, spotless and gleaming.

When the work was finally done, the city looked like a dream.

But was it?

The king set out for a royal tour of his new paradise. Everywhere he looked, the beauty was breathtaking. The golden domes reflected the morning sun. The gardens stretched endlessly, fragrant with the scent of jasmine and roses.

But something felt … wrong.

The usually lively streets were quiet. The laughter of merchants, the songs of farmers and the chatter of children were all gone.

The king frowned. 'Where are my people?'

His ministers exchanged nervous glances. The few villagers he did see walked with their heads lowered. Their eyes held no joy, no admiration for the grand city. Instead, they looked … worried. A fruit seller sat alone, her baskets barely touched. A child beside her clutched his stomach, too tired to cry. Further down, a man hammered a 'For Sale' sign onto his door. It was the third house on that street to be sold that week. A group of children peeked into the fountain, not to admire it but because they hoped someone might drop a coin in.

The city was beautiful. But it hid hunger. Why?

The king turned to Tenali Raman, his sharpest advisor. 'What is happening, Tenali?'

Tenali Raman stepped closer, his voice gentle but pointed. 'Your Majesty,' he said, 'if you could go back to the beginning ... what would you build first?'

NOW IMAGINE YOU WERE IN THE KING'S PLACE. WHAT WOULD YOU CHOOSE TO BUILD FIRST IN YOUR DREAM CITY?
- A golden palace that touches the clouds?
- A marketplace full of joy and laughter?
- Homes for every family?
- A place where art, music and stories come alive?

Tenali stroked his chin, glancing at the spotless streets.

'Your Majesty,' he said, 'would you call a tree beautiful if its roots were starving? Come, let us ask the roots themselves.'

The villager bowed low. 'Your Majesty ... the city is beautiful, but we are struggling. We sold grain, tools and even wedding bangles to pay the tax.' His voice trembled. 'Some eat only once every two days. Some not at all. We see gold everywhere ... except in our homes.'

The king looked around. He no longer saw marble and gold. He saw tired eyes, worn hands and homes hollowed by sacrifice.

Without another word, he stood tall and made a decision. 'The heavy taxes will be lifted immediately,' he declared.

A wave of relief and joy swept through the city like fresh rain after a drought. That night, for the first time in weeks, music played in the streets again. Families laughed, markets bustled and the city truly came alive.

And as King Krishnadevaraya stood on his palace balcony, watching lanterns float into the sky and hearing the hum of joy rising from his people, he smiled.

It was no longer just a city of gold. It was a city of hearts.

Common Sense, Uncommon Wins!

When sharp thinking
trumps shiny swords.

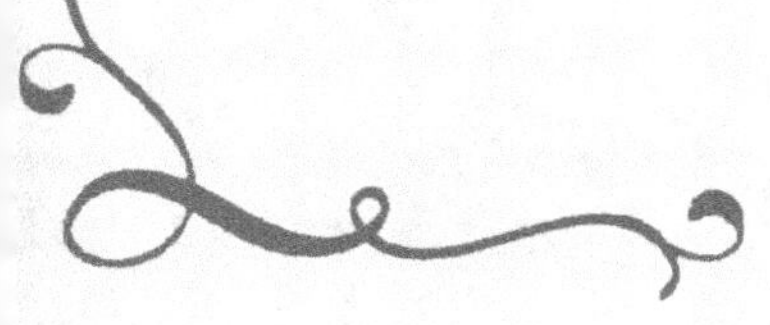

24

Death Sentence and the Great Escape

Long before Tenali Raman became King Krishnadevaraya's most trusted advisor, he was known for his mischievous tricks. Most of the time, his cleverness delighted the king. But one day, he went too far. Krishnadevaraya sat fuming on his throne, his face red with anger.

'Tenali Raman!' he thundered. 'You have broken palace rules, and for this, you shall be sentenced to death!'

Silence reigned, more absolute than any decree. Tenali, for once, did not laugh or smile. The guards seized him immediately. The execution was set. They dragged him to the execution grounds where the royal swordsmen stood, their blades gleaming under the sun.

'Prepare for your last moments,' a guard said grimly.

But Tenali was not ready to die so easily.

Tenali sighed dramatically, shaking his head. 'Wait!' he said, his voice quivering. 'I am a Brahmin,' he announced. 'I am not afraid to die, but I must first perform my final rituals.'

The guards exchanged glances.

'Please,' Tenali continued, placing his hands together in prayer. 'Let me bathe and complete my sacred rites before I leave this world.'

The executioners, respecting religious customs, nodded solemnly. They led him to the palace lake, where he bathed and performed his prayers. The sun dipped lower in the sky.

Just as the guards were about to take him back, Tenali sighed deeply again. 'Now,' he said, placing a hand on his stomach, 'I must eat my final meal.'

The soldiers, believing this was his last wish, brought him food. Tenali ate slowly. Very, very slowly.

The guards grew impatient. 'Are you done yet?' one of them snapped.

Tenali licked his fingers thoughtfully. 'Hmm ... yes, yes. Now, I must complete one last ritual.'

The executioners exchanged exasperated looks.

'What now?' one of them asked.

Tenali smiled innocently. 'Oh dear! I nearly forgot,' he gasped. 'I must now sing my farewell song.'

NOW IMAGINE YOU WERE ONE OF THE GUARDS THAT DAY. WHAT WOULD YOU HAVE DONE?

* Insisted on following orders, no matter what?
* Got swept up in rituals, out of respect or confusion?
* Or paused to wonder: Is this man stalling ... or staging the cleverest escape in history?

And before anyone could react, Tenali took off running!

His feet barely touched the ground as he dashed into the palace gardens. By the time the guards realised what had happened, he was long gone! They searched everywhere, but Tenali Raman was untraceable. When King Krishnadevaraya heard what had happened, he did something no one expected.

He laughed heartily. 'A man this clever does not deserve to die,' he declared.

And so, Tenali Raman lived on, not only to entertain and outwit everyone, but also to prove that wit can be sharper than a sword.

25

The Magic Chant

A dark shadow loomed over Vijayanagara.

Thieves were running wild, slipping through the streets like whispers in the wind. No matter how many guards were posted, how many warnings were issued, nothing could stop them.

King Krishnadevaraya paced in his royal chamber, frustration clear on his face. 'Tenali!' he called. 'These thieves must be stopped! If my wealthiest merchants feel unsafe, what hope is there for the common people?'

Tenali stroked his chin, his sharp eyes glinting with an idea. 'Leave it to me, Your Majesty,' he said with a grin.

The next morning, a very unusual rumour spread through the kingdom.

'Have you heard? Seth Lakshmichand, the richest merchant in Vijayanagara, has learnt a magic chant from a powerful guru!'

WHAT WOULD YOU DO IF YOU HEARD SUCH A TALE?
* Would you trust it?
* Try it?
* Laugh it off?

'What does it do?' asked a curious spice trader.

'They say,' a silk merchant whispered, 'if he recites it, his treasury room will be completely protected, even if he leaves his doors wide open all night.'

And so, word of the magic chant spread. Gasps echoed through the market. A treasury room left unguarded? A room full of gold and jewels? The news travelled fast. And, as expected, it reached the ears of the thieves. That night, the thieves gathered in the shadows outside Lakshmichand's house.

'Magic chant or no magic chant,' one thief smirked, 'gold is still gold.'

They crept closer, their hands itching to snatch their fortune.

Lakshmichand had done exactly as Tenali instructed. He left his treasury room open, doors wide apart, as if begging to be looted.

The thieves exchanged grins. 'Easy pickings,' they whispered.

They tiptoed inside. They grabbed sacks of gold and escaped into the night. Or so they thought. By the time they reached their hiding place, something felt … strange.

'What's on your hands?' one thief muttered.

The others looked down. Dark paint. On their hands. On their feet.

'What is this sorcery!' another thief yelped.

Little did they know, their own footprints had left behind a perfect trail leading all the way to their hideout. Before they could scrub it off, torches blazed in the distance.

GUARDS!

Within minutes, the thieves were caught red-handed, or rather, black-footed! And where did the trail lead? Right to Manilal's house, a former courtier who had been secretly helping them.

The next morning, the royal court buzzed with excitement as the captured thieves were brought before the king.

King Krishnadevaraya raised an eyebrow at Tenali. 'Tenali, tell me, why did Lakshmichand leave his treasury doors open? Wasn't that reckless?'

Tenali chuckled. 'Not at all, Your Majesty! I instructed him to apply fresh dark paint on the floor before nightfall.'

The court leaned in, intrigued.

'The moment the thieves stepped inside, they unknowingly walked on the wet paint. As they escaped, they left a perfect trail leading straight to their hideout.'

There was a moment of stunned silence. The king threw his head back and laughed. 'Tenali, you have once again proven that wit is stronger than magic!'

As the court cheered, Tenali bowed dramatically. The king awarded him a diamond ring. The thieves were locked away.

And as for the people of Vijayanagara? They learnt a valuable lesson that day: no magic chant could ever outsmart the wit of Tenali Raman.

26

The Sandalwood Fragrance

The royal court of Vijayanagara hummed with whispers.

A group of courtiers, their eyes filled with jealousy, huddled together. 'Your Majesty,' one of them finally spoke, 'Tenali Raman has grown arrogant. He hasn't even arrived today. Perhaps he thinks he is too important to serve the court!'

Another nodded. 'He hasn't solved any great problem in weeks! Maybe he's losing his cleverness.'

The king leaned back, observing their smug expressions. He knew that jealousy spoke louder than truth. Before he could respond, the guards announced a visitor.

A trader entered, carrying a bundle of sandalwood incense sticks. His robes were dusty with travel, but his eyes gleamed with confidence.

He bowed. 'Your Majesty, I bring you the finest incense from a distant land. Its fragrance is unmatched.'

Intrigued, the king leaned forward. 'What is the price for these sticks?'

The trader smiled knowingly. 'Just two hands full of smoke, Your Majesty.'

The courtiers exchanged confused glances.

'Two hands full of smoke?' one of them scoffed. 'How absurd!'

'Who asks for something that cannot be held?' another sneered.

The trader remained calm. 'Your Majesty, your court is famous for its wisdom. Surely, someone here can figure it out.'

The ministers straightened their robes, eager to prove their intellect. One reached out, trying to catch the smoke in his hands. Another waved his arms in the air, attempting to trap it between his palms. A third tried to cup the smoke into a golden bowl.

But no matter what they did, the smoke slipped through their fingers, leaving them looking ridiculous. The king chuckled at their foolish attempts.

The trader merely shook his head. 'Perhaps,' he mused, 'your court is not as wise as I had heard '

The ministers flushed with embarrassment. Just then, the doors swung open. Tenali Raman walked in confidently.

The king, still amused, repeated the trader's challenge. 'Tenali,' he said, 'can you give this man two hands full of smoke?'

IF SOMEONE CHALLENGED YOU TO GIVE THEM TWO HANDS FULL OF SMOKE, HOW WOULD YOU SOLVE IT?
* Would you try to trap it in a jar?
* Would you argue that it's impossible?

Tenali nodded thoughtfully. 'Give me a moment, Your Majesty.'

The courtiers smirked. Even Tenali wouldn't be able to solve this. But Tenali simply walked out of the courtroom. A few moments later, he returned carrying an iron pipe and a small velvet bag.

The court leaned in, watching.

Tenali lit an incense stick, allowing the fragrant smoke to fill the iron pipe. Once it was full, he sealed one end and carefully tied the velvet bag around the other.

Then, with great ceremony, he handed the bag to the trader. 'Here,' he said. 'Two hands full of smoke. Be careful. It's valuable.'

For a moment, there was silence. Then, the trader burst into laughter.

'Your Majesty,' he said, shaking his head in admiration, 'I had heard of Tenali Raman's wit, but today I see it with my own two eyes!'

'Indeed, Tenali! Once again, you have outsmarted us all,' the king said, before removing a diamond ring from his finger and placing it in Tenali's palm.

Tenali tucked the ring into his pocket and said, 'A little smoke, a lot of thinking and a trader's ego has finally cooled down.'

'Perhaps next time,' he continued lightly, 'our friends in the court should be careful before saying that I am of no use.'

The trader left with a velvet bag of smoke. And the court was left with the scent of cleverness in the air.

27

Climbing Out of Trouble

One afternoon, the grand court of Vijayanagara was filled with tension.

King Krishnadevaraya sat on his throne, his expression dark with anger. 'Enough, Tenali!' he thundered. 'You have crossed the line this time. Leave my kingdom immediately!'

Everyone knew that arguing with the king in this mood was a terrible idea. But Tenali Raman? He simply bowed, smiled faintly and walked out of the palace without a word.

Days passed.

The king's anger cooled, but he remained firm in his decision. Tenali was gone. Then, one morning, while out on a horseback ride through the royal forest, the king spotted something unusual. A figure was scrambling up a tree, climbing higher and higher with surprising speed.

The king squinted. Who could it be?

He urged his horse forward, stopping beneath the tree. He looked up. And there, perched on a high branch, was none other than Tenali Raman!

The king's face darkened. 'Tenali,' he bellowed. 'Why are you still here? I ordered you to leave my kingdom.'

Tenali, balancing carefully, looked down and grinned. 'Your Majesty, I tried! I truly tried.'

The king folded his arms, waiting. 'I walked for miles, crossed rivers and ventured beyond the borders. But no matter where I went, I was still in your dominion. Every village, every road, every corner of the land, it all belongs to you!'

The king raised an eyebrow. 'So?'

Tenali stretched his arms dramatically. 'So, I had only one option left. Since I cannot leave your kingdom on earth, I thought I should try heading to heaven instead!'

WHAT WOULD YOU DO IF EVERY PATH OUT OF TROUBLE STILL LED BACK TO THE SAME PROBLEM?
* Would you run farther?
* Plead harder?
* Or ... climb a tree and make the skies your ally?

For a moment, there was silence. Then, King Krishnadevaraya roared with laughter. The ministers, guards and even royal attendants, they all chuckled at Tenali's wit.

The king shook his head, wiping away his amusement. 'You trickster!' he said. 'Get down from there before you break your neck.'

Tenali climbed down slowly, dusting off his clothes.

The king sighed, his anger completely gone. 'Fine, you win. Stay in Vijayanagara. I should have known that wherever my kingdom is, my court jester is never far behind.'

Tenali grinned. 'And wherever my king is, trouble never stays far behind either!'

The king chuckled. 'Only you would try to climb into heaven to avoid exile.'

28

How to Win a Spot by the Fireside

The night was dark, rain poured in heavy sheets and winds howled through the trees like restless spirits.

Soaked from head to toe, Tenali Raman trudged towards a roadside inn, hoping to find warmth. Inside, a group of villagers huddled around the only fireplace, their hands stretched towards the flickering flames.

Tenali shivered, rubbing his arms. 'Excuse me,' he said, 'could I squeeze in by the fire?'

But the villagers barely spared him a glance. 'No room,' one muttered.

'Find another spot,' said another, without moving an inch.

IF YOU WERE IN TENALI'S PLACE HOW WOULD YOU RESPOND?

♣ Would you beg them to let you in?

♣ Would you wait in the cold, hoping someone moves?

♣ Or would you come up with a clever trick to make them leave?

Tenali sighed dramatically, shaking the water from his sleeves. 'Oh dear,' he muttered loudly, 'what a terrible night! And to make things worse, I seem to have lost my purse nearby. It had … oh, about twenty gold coins in it.'

The room fell silent. The men near the fire sat up straight.

'Twenty gold coins?' one whispered.

'Nearby?' another repeated.

Then, all of a sudden, the crowd seemed to part! People jumped to their feet and rushed out in the storm, their lanterns swinging wildly. The wind shrieked. The rain pelted down. But none of it mattered. All they could think about was finding the golden treasure waiting for them in the mud.

Tenali smiled, stretched his hands towards the now-empty fireplace and sighed contentedly. 'Ahh, that's better,' he said, basking in the warmth.

The landlord, watching the whole scene unfold, chuckled.

'You tricked them well, Tenali.'

WHAT DO YOU THINK?
- ♣ Was it wrong of Tenali to trick them? Or was it fair, since they were selfish first?
- ♣ Would you have fallen for his trick?

Tenali smirked. 'They were greedy,' he replied. 'But don't worry, they'll be back by morning, colder, wetter and a little wiser.'

And just as he predicted, by dawn, the villagers stumbled back in, shivering and empty-handed.

But by then, Tenali Raman had already enjoyed a warm, restful night by the fire.

29

A Coin for the King's Face

One evening, Tenali Raman walked out of the royal court, his mind still occupied with the day's discussions. As he reached into his pocket, a single copper coin slipped from his fingers and landed on the ground with a soft clink.

Tenali immediately bent down and began searching for it. Just then, Rajguru, his longtime rival, happened to pass by.

He smirked, then turned to King Krishnadevaraya, who was watching from a distance. 'Your Majesty, look at him! You have showered Tenali with riches, yet he's scrambling around for a single copper coin? How greedy!'

Tenali, without missing a beat, stood up, dusted off his hands, and bowed respectfully before the king. 'Oh no, Your

Majesty,' he said smoothly. 'I am not searching for the coin because of its value.'

He paused for effect, then added with a knowing smile, 'One side of that coin has your face on it. I cannot bear the thought of people trampling on it!'

The echo of the last line lingered. Then, laughter erupted! King Krishnadevaraya laughed heartily and shook his head. 'Tenali, your words are as valuable as gold! If you respect my face so much, let me reward you properly.'

And with that, he gifted Tenali a diamond ring, far more valuable than the lost copper coin. Rajguru, standing nearby, fumed in silence. Once again, Tenali had turned an insult into an opportunity.

A copper coin was lost. But Tenali's wit, as always, came back richer.

WHAT DO YOU THINK?

♣ Can you think of a comeback as witty as Tenali's? Try it! Imagine someone teasing you for something small. What would your witty reply be?

30

Half Sun, Half Shade

One afternoon, Tenali Raman made a light-hearted joke about the king's sense of humour.

But King Krishnadevaraya, not in the mood for laughter, took offence. His face darkened, and his voice boomed across the court. 'Enough of your jokes, Tenali! Leave my kingdom immediately!'

The courtiers were startled. One minister dropped his fan in surprise. Some of them, secretly jealous of Tenali, smirked in satisfaction. At last, the king's favourite jester was gone.

Days passed. Then weeks.

At first, the court felt peaceful without Tenali's constant mischief. But soon, something felt … missing. The king's ministers struggled with decisions. His advisors lacked quick wit. The court had become dull.

Krishnadevaraya sighed, resting his chin on his hand. 'I may have been too harsh,' he muttered. 'Tenali's wit was annoying, but it also solved problems. I need him back.'

But how could he call back Tenali without admitting he had been wrong? Then, an idea struck him.

The next morning, the king announced a strange challenge. 'I will reward anyone who can appear before me standing in both sunlight and shade at the same time.'

The court buzzed with whispers.

'Sun and shade together?'

'That's impossible!'

'How can one be in both at once?'

For days, people tried. Some carried mirrors to reflect sunlight. Others stood under tree branches, but that wasn't true shade. No one could get it right.

WHAT WOULD YOU HAVE DONE?
- ♣ If the king gave you a challenge that seemed impossible, would you have tried to outthink the sun itself?
- ♣ Or would you look at the world a little sideways, like Tenali always did?

Then, on the fourth day, a man arrived carrying a woven basket over his head.

He stood before the king, smiling confidently. 'Your Majesty,' he said, 'I am standing in half sun and half shade.'

A flicker of disbelief danced in the king's eyes.

A basket? Of course! The tiny holes in the weave let in specks of sunlight while still casting a shadow.

The king let out a raucous laugh. 'Only one man could have devised this! Call Tenali back at once!' And just like that, Tenali Raman was welcomed back into the court, not as a fool, but as the one man the king simply couldn't do without. Sometimes, wit shines brighter than the sun, even in the shade.

31

The New Bridge

One evening, as the sun cast golden streaks across the sky, King Krishnadevaraya posed a simple yet puzzling question to his court. 'What is the best season of all?'

The grand court of Vijayanagara buzzed with debate.

'Spring!' declared one minister. 'The air is fresh, the flowers bloom and life feels renewed.'

'Winter!' argued another. 'The cool breeze is pleasant, and it is the perfect time for grand feasts and celebrations.'

Some spoke of summer's bounty, others of autumn's beauty.

Then, Tenali Raman raised his hand. 'Your Majesty,' he said, 'the rainy season is the best of all.'

The court nodded thoughtfully, considering his words. But just as they were about to agree, Tenali added something surprising. 'And it is also the worst season of all.'

'How can it be both?' someone muttered.

The king, amused, leaned forward. 'Prove it, Tenali.'

A sly smile played on Tenali's lips.

'Give me a month, Your Majesty. I will show you.'

A few weeks later, the monsoon arrived in full force. The sky turned a deep shade of grey, and the scent of fresh earth filled the air as raindrops danced on the rooftops.

One afternoon, the king decided to take a pleasure ride into the jungle.

His royal entourage, comprising his ministers, courtiers and guards rode through the misty forest, their horses splashing through muddy paths. The journey was beautiful. The lush green leaves glistened with raindrops, the streams overflowed with crystal-clear water and peacocks danced in the distance.

'Truly,' the king murmured, 'the rainy season is magical.'

But nature had other plans.

Dark clouds rolled in. The wind howled. And suddenly rain poured down in torrents. The peaceful streams they had crossed earlier swelled into raging rivers. The court found itself trapped on the wrong side of a now-flooded stream. The once-dry bed was now a churning force of water, blocking their way home.

Ministers panicked. Guards shouted.

'We must turn back!' one yelled.

'We are stranded!' cried another.

The king, though calm, felt uneasy. The waters were too dangerous to cross. And just then, a lone woodcutter appeared.

The king's eyes lit up. 'You there!' he called. 'Can you help us?'

The woodcutter nodded silently and set to work. Using fallen branches, strong vines and sheer determination, he built a makeshift bridge over the raging stream.

One by one, the royal party cautiously stepped across. The bridge held firm. Finally, as the last person stepped onto safe ground, the woodcutter removed his disguise.

The court gasped. 'Tenali Raman!'

The king burst into laughter. 'Now I see your point!' he exclaimed. 'The rainy season makes the world beautiful, but it also brings trouble.'

Tenali bowed with a grin. 'Exactly, Your Majesty. Every season has two sides, just like life. Joy and hardship go hand in hand.'

The king, still chuckling, turned to his ministers. 'From now on, we shall ensure that proper bridges are built before the monsoon arrives.'

And so, thanks to Tenali's shrewd lesson, the kingdom prepared better for the rainy season, and no one was stranded again.

WHAT ABOUT YOU?

* What is your favourite season?
* Is it your favourite because it is good? Or does it have challenges too?

Epilogue

As the years passed, Tenali Raman's wit and wisdom made him a legend in the Vijayanagara court. But with great intelligence came great jealousy. Courtiers, ministers and even the Rajguru, the royal priest envied his influence over King Krishnadevaraya. And so, they schemed.

But behind all of Tenali's playful antics was something deeper, a devotion that even the king didn't notice.

You see, even jesters have their sacred moments. The courtiers had noticed something peculiar. Every morning, Tenali would slip into an upstairs room and lock the door from within. He stayed there for hours, undisturbed. His wife and mother never questioned it, but over time, the household servants took notice. They whispered among themselves, and soon the rumours found their way to the royal court.

'What could he be hiding?' the ministers whispered among themselves.

'Perhaps he is counting stolen jewels!'

'Or meeting with spies!'

They saw their chance when Tenali was away from court one day. They rushed to the king, feeding his mind with suspicion. 'Your Majesty, Tenali Raman keeps a room locked at all times. Shouldn't we find out what's inside?'

IF YOUR TRUSTED ADVISER GREW SECRETIVE, WHAT WOULD YOU DO?
* Doubt their loyalty?
* Or wait and watch with patience?

Krishnadevaraya, though a just ruler, was human after all. He grew curious. But unlike the ministers, he did not want to investigate in Tenali's absence.

'No,' he said, his eyes sharp. 'We will go when he is inside. Let him explain himself.'

Before sunrise the next day, the king and his courtiers arrived unannounced at Tenali's house. His wife and mother were startled. They bowed respectfully, but before they could alert Tenali, the king gestured for silence.

With a swift command, the ministers barged into the upstairs room, eager to expose Tenali. Inside, they expected gold, stolen treasures or secret letters from enemy spies.

But instead, they found something strange. A dimly lit room, fragrant with incense. A picture of Goddess Kali stood before them, surrounded by fresh flowers. A plain mat lay on the ground, next to a chart of yoga asanas. And in the middle of the room, seated cross-legged in deep meditation, was Tenali Raman. He wore an old, tattered dhoti, washed but worn with time.

Krishnadevaraya gently shook him awake.

Tenali opened his eyes slowly, saw the king, and smiled. 'Your Majesty, what brings you here at this hour?'

The king looked around. 'What do you do here, Tenali? And why this old dhoti?'

Tenali folded his hands and spoke with humility.

'This is the dhoti I wore the first time I visited the Kali temple in my hometown. I do not want to forget where I come from. Every morning, I spend time in prayer and meditation, because no matter how wise a man becomes, he is nothing without grace from god. The Divine Mother protects me more than any king or kingdom ever could.'

Krishnadevaraya nodded thoughtfully.

The courtiers, who had expected to see greed and deception, now stood speechless before Tenali's devotion and simplicity. They lowered their heads, ashamed of their jealousy.

Years passed, and Tenali Raman's fame only grew. His wit, wisdom and laughter filled the courts of Vijayanagara. His stories spreading far beyond its walls.

One evening, as he walked through the temple gardens, he paused under a grand neem tree, watching the golden hues of the sunset bathe the city he had served for so long. A soft breeze whispered through the leaves, carrying echoes of the laughter, debates and playful banter that had once filled the royal court.

A young boy, no older than ten, ran up to him and asked, 'Tenali uncle, will you tell me one of your stories?'

Tenali chuckled, patting the boy's head. 'Of course, my child. But first, promise me something.'

'What?' the boy asked eagerly.

'That you will never stop asking questions. That you will always look for answers, not just in books, but in the world around you. That you will use your wit to help others.'

The boy nodded, eyes wide with wonder.

And so, under the setting sun, Tenali Raman told yet another tale.

And that's how his story never truly ended. For even today, his wit makes us laugh. Even today, his wisdom makes us think. And even today, in every curious mind and clever heart, Tenali Raman lives on.

Acknowledgements

I offer my heartfelt gratitude to Daaji, my beloved guru. He was the first person who told me I should write stories and books for children, the first to see that potential in me, even before I saw it in myself. His presence, his wisdom and his storytelling have shaped my spirit and my pen in ways too vast to measure.

To my mother, for being the centre of my world. She is the most compassionate person I have ever known. She has been the silent architecture of my courage. Without her, I might have crumbled long ago.

To my father, who unknowingly made me a storyteller. As a child, I wouldn't eat dinner unless he fed me with a new story. But there was a rule: he was never allowed to repeat a story. So, night after night, year after year, he had a story—original, funny and wise. I don't know if he made them up on the spot or drew from memory. I grew up thinking this was normal parenting. Only much later did I realise how special dinner time was and how quietly remarkable my father was. These memories curled up in a warm corner of my heart, waiting to be reawakened later.

To my husband, my unwavering companion for the past two decades, who kept telling me again and again that I was meant to be a published author. His encouragement has been as steady as his love, and I know that in every version of every lifetime that has been, he was my first reader and my last listener.

To my son, who would say to me just before bedtime, 'Amma, tell me a story.' The rule was: no repeats. Twenty years later, long after he had left for college, I asked him, 'What's your favourite childhood memory?' he said, 'You told me stories every night before I fell asleep. You did not repeat a single one. How do you know 6,000 unique stories?' The funny part is, I don't. But then, we don't *tell* stories. We *live* stories. We live eight billion stories in this world. And we become what we believe our stories are.

I also realised that I was standing in my father's shoes. I am sure my son's son or daughter is going to give him the same feeling. And I am sure many, many people think this of their own parents and grandparents. That's the magic of stories passed from heart to heart.

So, to all the keepers of oral tradition—parents, grandparents, schoolteachers and storytellers who have carried forward Tenali Raman's tales and other stories across generations, you are the original custodians of wisdom wrapped in humour and love.

To my friends, you know who you are. And you know why I'm thanking you. You stood with me through my hardest seasons and never let me be swallowed by them. You sat with me until I could rise again.

To my editor and one of my closest friends, Vidhi, thank you for your confidence, love and friendship, and certainly your expertise as an editor.

To my publishing team, for bringing this work to fruition, and putting the young reader first.

To the readers, young and old, who continue to love Tenali Raman. I hope this book makes you laugh, makes you think and maybe even makes you tell your own stories.

To Tenali Ramakrishna himself, for your wit that still disarms, your wisdom that still guides, and the way your stories continue to heal, inspire and help us shape the narratives through which we remember who we truly are.

And finally to all of us. These stories are for children. But they are also for the child in all of us.

Thank you,
Purnima Ramakrishnan

About the Author

Purnima Ramakrishnan writes for both grown-ups and children. Her work has appeared in *The Huffington Post*, *Shot@Life*, and the Gates Foundation's *Impatient Optimists*. But what she enjoys most is writing for young readers— stories that invite laughter, spark reflection, and sometimes leave a quiet pause behind.

Purnima didn't always write stories. She studied electronics and began her career in the automotive industry. Then one day, she started listening closely to the real stories people live every day. That listening led her to writing—and writing took her to places she had never imagined. From Brazil, as a fellow of the International Reporting Project, to the United Nations stage, where she received the Elizabeth Neuffer Prize for her reporting, her everyday stories helped bring distant lives into a shared narrative.

She now lives in India with her family and is also a heartfulness meditation trainer. She runs Heartfulness Institute (heartfulness.org), and her practice continues to shape the calm, thoughtful voice of her writing. She believes that telling stories, and listening to them, has the power to change us—slowly at first, then all at once.